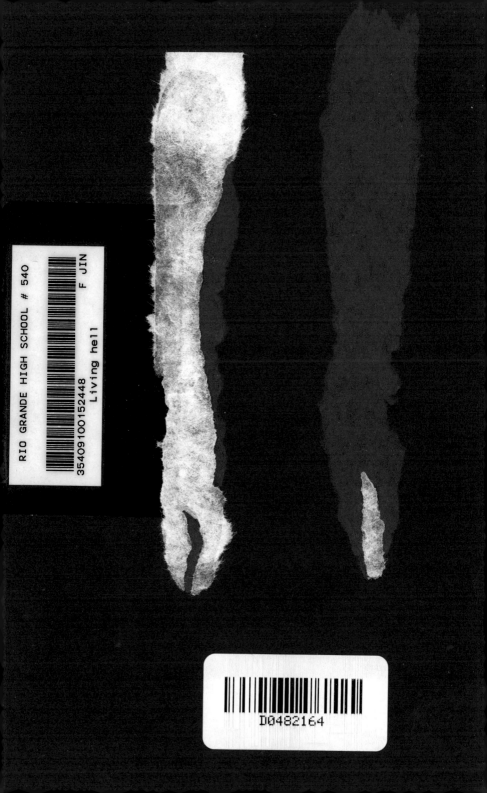

RIO GRANDE HIGH SCHOOL # 540
F JIN
3540910015244
Living hell

D0482164

[Living Hell]

Living Hell

< Catherine Jinks >

Harcourt

Houghton Mifflin Harcourt

Boston   New York   2010

// Also by Catherine Jinks //

< www.catherinejinks.com >

o

<Copyright © 2007 by Catherine Jinks>

[All rights reserved. For information about permission to reproduce
selections from the work, write to Permissions, Houghton Mifflin
Harcourt Publishing Company, 215 Park Avenue South, New York,
New York 10003.]

<First published in 2007 in Australia by Allen & Unwin.
First U.S. edition 2010.>

\\ Harcourt is an imprint of Houghton Mifflin Harcourt
Publishing Company. \\

<www.hmhbooks.com>

\\ Text set in Apollo MT \\

Library of Congress Cataloging-in-Publication Data
Jinks, Catherine.
Living hell / Catherine Jinks. —1st U.S. ed.
p. cm.
Summary: Chronicles the transformation of a spaceship into a
living organism, as seventeen-year-old Cheney leads the hundreds
of inhabitants in a fight for survival while machines turn on them,
treating all humans as parasites.
ISBN 978-0-15-206193-7 (hardcover : alk. paper) [1. Space ships—
Fiction. 2. Survival — Fiction. 3. Science fiction.] I. Title.
PZ7.J5754Liv 2010
[Fic]—dc22
2009018938

<Manufactured in the United States of America>

FFG   10 9 8 7 6 5 4 3 2 1
4500210492

< To Peter and Hannah, with love >

[Living Hell]

Chapter One

You have to understand what it was like.

There were so many of us—hundreds and hundreds. In A Crew alone there were more than seven hundred people. And B Crew was almost as big. Not that we had anything to do with B Crew. But they were there, in the Stasis Banks. Ready for their next shift.

The shift that never arrived.

Back then, I didn't know everyone's name. There were too many names to remember. We could do all sorts of things, because we had the numbers. We played sports. We held concerts. We threw parties. You won't believe this, but at the very instant our probe detected that emission wave, I was attending a birthday party. Haemon Goh's ninth birthday party.

In those days there were all kinds of nicknames. Haemon was a Shifter, just like me, because he had been born on board *Plexus* during one of A Crew's shifts. I was a Second Shifter, and he was a Fourth Shifter. You won't understand about shifts. Each of them was four years long, because cytopic stasis isn't supposed to last more than four years. Any longer and you can suffer permanent damage. So every four years there would be a change of personnel as one crew woke up and the other was put into suspension.

It means that I'm older than I look. The day it happened—the day everything changed forever—I was seventeen. But only in shift years. If you're talking real time, I was thirty-three. Haemon was turning nine, but he was really seventeen. We were on our sixth shift, you see. The last month of the second year of our sixth shift, after forty-six years in space.

And we still hadn't found a habitable planet.

Not that it mattered much—not then. Not to us. The Shifters had never been on Earth. We didn't know what planets were like. *Plexus* was self-contained and self-sustaining. It gave us everything we wanted; it was designed to satisfy our every need. How could we miss what we'd never known? My parents might have pined occasionally, but I never did. No Shifter, to my knowledge, ever had to be counseled for a bout of ship fever, because we didn't understand what it was like to walk under an open sky or feel a cool breeze. Not really. There were programs, of course: virtual reproductions that allowed you to look up at the clouds or roll on the grass. Our teachers would sometimes take us to the Mimexis Chamber for a sensory experience of Earth. But mimexis wasn't the same as reality. There was always a kind of buzz at the corners of your perception, like interference in an electromagnetic energy stream. You always knew that it was fake.

((2))

As a matter of fact, Haemon's parents had booked the Mimexis Chamber for his birthday party. That happened a lot, as I recall. Mimexis was popular for birthday parties. It wasn't easy to book a session unless you were mapping a galaxy cluster or teaching a class . . . or throwing a birthday party. It wasn't as if you could just stroll into the chamber whenever you wanted to go to the beach. Mimexis wasn't "energy-efficient"; we were told that all the time. There had to be a damn good reason for powering up those laser coils. Luckily, a Shifter birthday was considered important enough.

I remember Haemon's party so well. There were fireworks—*virtual* fireworks—and a million balloons, and a snowstorm, and the Undersea Tour. I had been on that tour before; like the Black Hole tour, and the Human Body tour, and the Ancient Rome tour, it was part of our curriculum. But Haemon wasn't old enough to have studied marine biology, so the tour was new to him, and he enjoyed it. He also enjoyed the cake, which was an impressive piece of design. Someone had written a new program and had created a cake so big that when it popped open, hundreds of virtual parakeets flew out, singing like blackbirds. We all chased them with butterfly nets. And when we caught them, they transformed into other things: flowers, bonbons, jewelery, ribbons. After that there was dancing. I don't know who chose the music. Some of it was all right, but some of it was Plexus Mix. Mixing your own music was quite popular in those days. One of the Third Shifters spent a lot of time tracking and sampling. He called it a hobby.

I won't tell you what Dygall called it.

Dygall was there, needless to say. Everyone eighteen or under

((3))

was expected to attend birthday parties, and most of us were happy to do so. I won't speak for Dygall—he was always griping about something, parties included—but the rest of us found parties an enjoyable duty. Even Caromy turned up, though she didn't need to. Perhaps, as First Born, she felt a certain responsibility toward every Shifter on *Plexus*.

She was twenty-one, then—forty-one in real-time years. I think she was working in Sustainable Services. (It's been so long, I can't remember.) She'd done something funny to her hair; it was twisted up into a couple of golden antennae, which bounced when she nodded and made Haemon laugh. Mostly she played with Haemon and the smaller kids: the Fourth and Fifth Shifters. It was the right thing to do. I wish I could have danced with her, though. Just once.

She was so beautiful and so good. She shone like a supernova.

Neither of the other two First Shifters had come. I wouldn't have expected them to; they weren't like Caromy. Of the Second Shifters, I was there and Merrit was there, but Yestin wasn't. He was in MedLab, undergoing blood tests. Poor Yestin was always trotting off to MedLab. He was the only Shifter born with a physical defect: Artificial Gravity Intolerance (AGI). Though every Shifter had been thoroughly screened before birth, there had been no methodology for AGI screening. No one had encountered it before. The gene mix hadn't been identified. The symptoms weren't properly understood. Everyone knew about the effects of zero gravity—the loss of muscle and bone mass, the pressure on the carotid artery, the slowing of the pulse—but when it came to artificial gravity, there hadn't been much research done.

Yestin changed all that. After he was born, a whole section of MedLab became devoted to gravimetrics, and Yestin spent many long hours there, having his osteoblast levels boosted, and his exercise programs adjusted, and his blood chemistry analyzed. The rest of the time he built robots. That was another popular pastime among the Shifters: building robots. I had built a few myself when I was younger. But I was never like Yestin. That kid was obsessed. He wasn't satisfied with miniature spacecraft or trick basketballs. He was determined to recreate dogs and cats and birds—robotic animals with random-probability patterning and chemical biosensors.

Given the chance, he probably would have moved on to the challenge of recreating a human being: a human being with sturdy bones made of strong metallic composites. But he didn't have time. For most of us, our future died on the day of that party.

I still like to think about it, though.

Who else was there? Haemon's parents, of course. His counselor. His personal trainer. His best friend, Inaret. (She was another Fourth Shift kid). His teacher, who was on the Psychologics staff and who was responsible for Junior School. Plus the Senior School teacher, who had awarded me a double-honors graduation just the year before. And that was about it, I think. Apart from the Shifters I haven't already named.

I remember, before the dancing, how everyone had been encouraged to draw patterns on their clothes with paint-pencils. (*Virtual* paint-pencils, naturally. There was no risk of staining anything.) Merrit, who was wearing navy blue, drew a star-chart. Caromy drew flowers and butterflies. Dygall drew a skeleton that he assured me was "anatomically correct." It wasn't, but I didn't argue. I had learned not to argue with Dygall. Just as Yestin was the only Shifter born with a physical defect, Dygall stood out as the one Shifter with a *character* defect. The fact is he liked to argue. Arguing allowed him to annoy people, and that was his hobby: annoying people. I used to talk to my counselor about Dygall—especially after I was appointed Dygall's Big Brother—because the kid worried me. What did he think he was up to? Why did he say (and do) such stupid things? Believe it or not, he had threatened to free all the germinators in BioLab. And to build a flame thrower. And to sabotage the Remote Access Laundry Units. (We called them RALs.) When I explained this to Teillo, my counselor, he just laughed. He said that all this behavior was typically adolescent. Whereupon I pointed out that no other adolescents on board exhibited such perverse and antisocial attitudes. Dygall, I said, was a destabilizing influence.

I'll never forget Teillo's reply. He told me that a bit of destabilization wasn't necessarily a bad thing. He said that *Plexus* was an "incredibly unnatural" setup. He observed, "It's all very well talking about stability, and counseling stability, and breeding for stability, but you can get too stable. What happens if we begin to stagnate? What happens if we find a new Earth but can't break out of the box we've built for ourselves? Someone like Dygall keeps us all on our toes. He gives us room to maneuver."

Teillo was a wise man—the wisest in Psychologics—so I tried to look at Dygall in a new way. I tried to think of him as a *planned factor,* even though I knew he had come as a shock. He certainly embarrassed his dad. Zennor was a Senate member, representing the Psychologics Executive Committee. That, no doubt, was why he had been granted breeding privileges in the first place. No one else could have persuaded the Senate that his wife, Darice, would make a suitable mother. Oh, she was brilliant in her chosen field. As a food technologist and scent technician, she had no equal. It was thanks to Darice that our diets became more and more varied. But she wasn't stable. Her personality was too obsessive—too perfectionist. Her work consumed her. She used to float about in a daze most of the time, though she was very sweet when she *did* snap out of it. Very sweet and very, very beautiful. I'm not surprised that Zennor loved her. I'm also not surprised that Dygall messed around with stink bombs. Thinking about it now, I realize that he would have done anything to attract her attention.

Dygall had shaved his head a few days before the birthday party. I can't remember why; maybe there wasn't a reason. Maybe he was bored. (He often talked about the boredom of life on *Plexus*. Then, to be annoying, he would say that a military coup would liven things up.) A pale, gingery fuzz was just beginning to cover his scalp on the day of the party. The younger kids found it quite fascinating. I remember how they would ask if they could touch it, and Dygall would suddenly drop to his knees and bark like a dog, or say, "Be careful. It's catching. Do you want your own hair to fall out?" I tried to head him off, but there was no way of knowing what Dygall would do next. One minute he would be running around in circles, popping virtual balloons; the next minute he would be sulking in a corner. It was very difficult for me. His unexpected responses threw the smaller kids off balance.

But when I complained to Merrit, she simply shrugged and said, "Consider it a compliment. They wouldn't have made the match if they thought you couldn't handle it."

Merrit was sixteen at the time. Psychologics had teamed her up with a bright and happy Little Sister who wasn't giving her much trouble at all. The worst you could say about Inaret was that she made a lot of noise.

I pointed this out.

"So, are you telling me that your getting Inaret *wasn't* a compliment?" I asked. "Because she's nice and easy?"

Merrit flashed me one of her looks. We were standing against a wall watching the smaller kids dance with a virtual octopus.

"Inaret is a great deal of work," she insisted.

"Are you kidding?"

"No."

"She's brilliant, Merrit. She has the highest IQ on board."

"You think *that's* easy to deal with?"

"For you? Yes." If Inaret had the highest IQ, Merrit probably had the second highest. She was a mathematical genius. Even before she left school, she was running stat checks for Planning and Projection. The instant she graduated, my father snapped her up. Her first Rotation Placement was with him in Navigation, where she had been impressing everyone with her insights into cataclysmic variables.

"Anyway, at least Inaret seems socially integrated," I remarked, studying the eight-year-old as she flung herself around—rather clumsily, for someone her age. (She perhaps wasn't as well coordinated as she could have been.) "Nice manners. Receptive. Cheerful."

"Well, of course she seems that way to *you*," Merrit retorted. "It's because she's trying so hard to impress."

"What do you mean?"

"Cheney." Merrit had a way of glancing at you out of the corners of her long dark eyes while her face remained expressionless. "You're not displaying much insight."

"Huh?"

"She thinks the world of you."

Sure enough, Merrit had hardly finished speaking when Inaret suddenly clattered to a halt in front of me. "Can you be a sun?" she asked.

"Pardon?"

"We're doing a solar-system dance," she explained confidently. "You can be a sun, and we'll be planets."

"Oh."

"It's a binary system," Inaret added, seizing my hand. I ended up swinging her around and around while Caromy did the same with Haemon. It occurred to me that, although Haemon was older, Inaret did seem to be taking the lead in most things. Watching her, I began to see what Merrit was talking about. Inaret was certainly very firm in her opinions.

Haemon, on the other hand, hardly ever opened his mouth.

"Inaret needs a lot of convincing," Merrit said dryly when I joined her again. "You can't just tell her to do things. You have to *persuade* her to do things."

"Well . . . that's good, isn't it?"

"Is it? I don't know. It wears me out."

"It's still better than Dygall."

"What's Dygall doing, anyway?"

Dygall had brought a silvery insulation sheet with him. He was trying to refract energy waves, thereby distorting the image of the octopus. Inaret laughed as its head bubbled to one side. Haemon blinked his round, dark eyes in consternation.

"Please don't mess with the program, Dygall," Dygall's teacher requested. "It has a knock-on effect."

"Don't you think a knock-on effect might be interesting?" was Dygall's response.

"Possibly. But you might frighten some of the little ones. The mimexis distinction still isn't clear, for them."

Naturally, Dygall wasn't pleased. He slouched over to where I was standing. "It's a coddle-fest," he complained. "Those kids *need* a bit of scaring. We all do."

"Is that so?" Merrit said blandly.

"Yes it is so. Otherwise, the first alien we run into, we'll all die of fright."

Merrit smiled. Dygall scowled.

"It's true!" he insisted. "We need a few mimexic monster programs. To toughen us up. We have to be *prepared*."

"We are prepared," I pointed out, as mildly as I could. "That's what Planning and Projection is for. All the possibilities have been taken into account."

Dygall snorted. I knew what he thought of P&P. According to Dygall, no colonization plan could be complete without guns.

He had said, over and over again, that security on board *Plexus* was a farce because there were no firearms of any description. He had even been caught downloading weaponry blueprints from the history database.

Teillo, I remember, had been very amused by this. "That boy," he'd said, chuckling, "is a genius at pushing buttons." In a funny sort of way I knew what he meant. For all Dygall's noise he had never actually *built* a flame thrower. Nor had he sabotaged a mimexis program or designed his own search-and-destroy robot. As I said, he liked annoying people. And one way of annoying people is to challenge their most deeply held beliefs.

No one would have been allowed to join A Crew if they had regarded violence as a solution to anything. Naturally, Dygall's attitude worried everybody. As for Dygall, I think he enjoyed all the extra counseling he received for his destabilizing tendencies. He always did like to be the center of attention.

"For my party," he suddenly declared, "I want a historical piece. The Battle of Waterloo or something."

Merrit rolled her eyes.

"Oh, I'm sure the little ones will love that," I remarked.

"The little ones won't be allowed in here," said Dygall. "It'll just be me and you and . . . I think you should come, too." He nodded at Merrit. "You're obviously bored."

"Is that so?"

"I can tell by your hair. Only a person who's very, very bored puts so much time and effort into a hairstyle."

Merrit had long, straight, black hair, which she wore in a complicated pattern of fine plaits. I think her mother used to arrange it for her. When I saw Merrit flush, I knew that Dygall had gone too far.

Merrit was rather sensitive, you see. She couldn't laugh things off—and she didn't know Dygall all that well. She didn't understand that he would say whatever popped into his mind. He was never intentionally cruel, I don't think. Just tactless and impatient.

"You're a good one to talk about boredom-related hairstyles," I said to him quickly. "How long did that lunar landscape on your own scalp take you to finish?"

Dygall put a hand to his head. "Next time," he replied with deep satisfaction, "I'm going to leave bits. I'm going to write my name in my hair."

And that was when reality intruded. Even as Dygall spoke, Firminus opened the chamber door. He approached Haemon's father, and they exchanged a few words.

Suddenly the program faded. We were all left standing in an empty beige-colored compartment.

"I'm sorry, everyone," said Firminus in his calm, dry voice, "but we're going to need this chamber. We have to run a few charts."

The little kids groaned. Merrit and I frowned at each other. Firminus worked in Navigation; he wouldn't have interrupted Haemon's birthday party to run a few star-charts unless our course required urgent analysis.

"Do you need me, Firminus?" Merrit inquired.

"Not at present, Merrit, thanks all the same." Clearly Firminus wasn't prepared to give us any more details. "I apologize for the interruption."

"Oh, we were nearly through," Haemon's mother replied. She sounded genuinely unconcerned. "Haemon's had a great time, haven't you, honey?"

Haemon smiled shyly and nodded. Like his mother, he was very sweet-natured. And he didn't know enough to be worried. None of us did at that stage.

We didn't realize it was the beginning of the end.

Chapter Two

Dad didn't come back to our cabin for supper that night.

We always used to eat supper together if we could—Dad, Mum, and me. Mum was very firm about that. Even though we could have ordered our rations from any food dispenser on *Plexus,* she insisted that each evening meal should be a "family" one. Looking back, I can see why. My parents were busy people. They were both Senate members. Dad was on the Navigation Executive Committee. Mum filled an identical role for MedLab. Unless they had a firm schedule and stuck to it, family time was likely to slip away from them.

Back then, of course, I didn't really appreciate this. Family life didn't interest me. I was seventeen; when I turned eighteen, I would receive my own cabin. Not a family cabin (the family cabins were quite large), but a cabin nonetheless. Sloan Molyneux, my designated Big Brother, already had his own cabin. He'd had it for two years. It wasn't one of the spares—it had actually belonged to a deceased crew member—but it was still wholly desirable, in my opinion. Of course, there wasn't much you could do to stamp your personality on any part of *Plexus*. Not if you hadn't boarded the ship with a few souvenirs from Earth. On *Plexus* there were very strict rules about property and very few personal possessions. Pointless energy consumption was also frowned on. That's why Sloan hadn't arranged any knickknacks beside his bed or installed a pretty picture on his Interface Array. But his cabin, despite its standard fixtures and fittings, still seemed to reflect his character—perhaps because his character was so calm and controlled.

As for me, I had plans for my cabin when I finally got one. I was going to grow a plant. (That was allowed, provided you cleared it with Sustainable Services.) I was also going to hang up my great-great-great-great-great-great-grandfather's wristwatch, which I would be receiving on my eighteenth birthday. And I was going to invite Caromy to inspect my new quarters. That was definite.

Perhaps when she saw that I had finally grown up, she would look at me in a different way.

On the day of Haemon's party, however, I was still living with my parents. Our cabin designation was C9A69 (cabin number nine, A deck, sixty-ninth street). Cross-passages joining the tubes were always called streets when I was young. As for the tubes, they were our highways. They contained the tracks for our On-board Transport Vehicles (OTVs), which used to carry us from one point to another around the entire circumference of the ship's drum. By slapping the little red panel at any junction where a street met up with a tube, you could make the next OTV that came along stop for you.

There were never any accidents involving OTVs. I once saw Yestin fall off a platform into the path of an oncoming vehicle, and it stopped instantly. That was when he was still having dizzy spells; after that my mother insisted that he stay well away from the platform edges unless accompanied by someone of superior height and weight. But he was safe enough, really. We all were. The long-range sensors on the OTVs—and their extraordinary hair-trigger braking mechanisms—ensured that no one was ever hit.

I think there were twenty On-board Transport Vehicles altogether: five for each tube. The port-tube OTVs traveled clockwise; the starboard-tube OTVs went counterclockwise. You could catch them continuously in either direction on both A and B decks. And if you wanted to get from the port to the starboard tube in a hurry, every street had a shuttle.

The street shuttles were like mini-OTVs. They weren't enclosed, though. And they didn't contain seats. They were just moving platforms with hand-grips. It's amazing to think how easy we had it then. Imagine! A special vehicle just to carry us from one end of a street to the other! Not that most of us used shuttles. We were supposed to walk as much as we could—and sometimes we even ran. Sometimes the younger Shifters would *race* the street shuttles, which weren't very fast. That was one of the attractions of racing, I guess: the fact that you would generally win if you were competing against a street shuttle.

It was always hard to stop the little kids from running in areas where they shouldn't have been running. They never paid attention to the signs that prohibited "non-designated activities" in residential pressure cells. But since some of the kids weren't old enough to read, I suppose you couldn't blame them entirely. You just had to keep reminding them, over and over again, until the message finally sank in.

Speaking of residential pressure cells, my family occupied a large cabin in an ideal spot. Haemon's family lived on our street. Yestin's family lived just above us, on B deck. Our cell wasn't far from pump station number two, with its air pump, its filtration pump, and its photosynthesis machines. Oh, and it didn't take us long to get to the Health Center, either. That was in an open deck cell, free of streets and bulkheads. On both decks of this pressure cell there were courts and gymnasiums and enough open space to run (because it was a designated area) and to kick a ball around.

Not that you could just wander in to play ball whenever you felt like it. Access to the Health Center was strictly rationed so that everyone received enough "free-motion" exercise time. Competitive sports took place on Sundays, and you could watch the games if you felt like it.

Everything had been carefully thought out for our comfort and convenience. I can hardly believe that now. I can hardly believe we were so important.

Why didn't I savor it while I could?

Anyway, when I arrived back from Haemon's party, my mother was already in our cabin. She was doing three things at once: loading the laundry dump, studying the Interface Array, and talking to someone at MedLab. In those days *Plexus* had a very complex communication system. You could log on to the Visual Interlink Network (VIN) wherever there was an Interface

Array, and the visual would pop up like a window on a wall. (We used to call it Vindow because of this portal effect.) There was also a voice patch sewn into the collar of every garment, which allowed you to talk to any person on board. The ID bands around our wrists did more than monitor our vital signs. Each one contained a genetic signature that served as a lock-in code. By tracking our genetic signatures, CAIP—our Core Artificial Intelligence Program—could route signals from one person to another.

"I'll have to go, Sadira. Cheney just walked in," my mother declared upon catching sight of me. "I'll talk to you tomorrow, after I've read that report. Linkdown." She signed off. "How was the party?"

"Good," I said. The three-dimensional diagram displayed on the family room Interface Array was labeled "Proopiomelano-cortin chain." Mum had obviously brought some work home with her. "We finished early. Firminus had to run some charts," I continued, and seated myself at the table. "Do you know why?"

"Some kind of anomaly, your father says." Mum went to the food dispenser and keyed in directives. "He won't be eating with us. He has to stay on the Bridge for now."

"Really?" I was surprised. "Is it an emergency?"

"Of course not. We'd be on red alert if it was."

"Is that curry?"

"I think so." Mum lifted the cover on the first tray and sniffed. "Yes. That's curry."

We ate our supper. Mum asked about the party, and I asked about Yestin, who hadn't been able to attend. According to Mum,

Yestin's artificial osteocytes weren't behaving quite like the real thing. "But we're sorting it out," she assured me.

Yestin's health was of great concern to my mother.

She was fifty-one then (seventy-five in real time), but she didn't look it. Her hair was still brown, straight and fine and cut in short wedges. Her voice was still strong, and her movements brisk and full of purpose. Though small, she had a dominating presence— perhaps because of her pale, penetrating eyes. She always wore red. Not that she had much choice, mind you. Our clothes came only in four colors: red, navy, black, and beige. But given even this small selection, my mother always, always wore red.

"My turn to clean up," she announced when she had finished, and jumped to her feet. She was one of those people who are constantly darting around like electrons. You didn't often see her sitting still, unless she was studying a cardiograph or something. (My father called her Comet.) "Weren't you going to play chess with your dad tonight?"

"I think so."

"You'll have to find someone else to play with, then."

"I think I'll visit Sloan. We missed our Hobnob because of the party."

"Are you sure he's not at work? Sadira was complaining how she never sees him anymore. He's always got his nose stuck in some petri dish . . ."

"I'll visit him at work, then."

Sloan and I met three times a week for an hour in the late afternoon. These sessions were part of our Brotherhood program. I always looked forward to my Hobnobs with Sloan.

My Hobnobs with Dygall, on the other hand, weren't so much fun.

"See if Sloan's found out anything from Firminus," my mother urged as I headed for the door. "About this anomaly, I mean. Your father was very vague."

"All right."

"Back by twenty-three hundred, Cheney."

"Yup. I know."

"And tell Sloan to give his mother a call, will you? I'm sick of having Sadira moan on about how she never sees him."

Sadira was a Medic, like my own mum. Firminus was Sloan's father. I don't know why Sadira and Firminus partnered up, because they were very different, but it was an inspired genetic splice. Sloan was the result, and he combined all the best features of each parent. Though tall and slim and well-organized like his dad, he wasn't as stiff or as finicky. Though he had his mother's heavy, lustrous hair and rich coloring, he never complained about anything. (Life wasn't ever *quite* good enough for Sadira.) Sloan had his father's high cheekbones but his mother's large eyes; his father's incisive brain but his mother's smooth voice. It made you wonder if someone had broken the genetic manipulation laws. How could someone so perfectly conceived have been produced by sheer chance? That's what I thought at the time, anyway.

In my opinion Sloan's only fault lay in the fact that he didn't think much of Caromy. Though I never heard him say a bad word about anyone, his tone when he spoke of Caromy was slightly dismissive. I got the feeling that he considered her a little less bright than most people on board.

((20))

Had it been anyone but Sloan, I might have wondered if jealousy played a part in this attitude. After all, Caromy was First Born while Sloan had come in second. But resentment like that would have been illogical, and Sloan was always logical. Always.

It was what I admired about him.

"Where are you, Sloan?" I inquired as I headed for the port tube. (I had called him up to pinpoint his location.) "Are you working?"

"I'm always working, Cheney. You know that."

"In BioLab?"

"In my cabin."

"We missed our Hobnob today. Because of the party."

"Yes, of course. You must tell me about the party. In great detail."

"Now, you mean?"

"Whenever you like."

So I went to visit Sloan in his cabin. Here I found him poring over some kind of slowly unfolding calculation on the Interface Array, surrounded by various oddly shaped, transparent vessels full of soupy jellies. I peered at these vessels one by one.

"How are the little guys?" I queried.

"Oh, thriving. No complaints."

"This one's new." I pointed.

"Not really. It's garden-variety *Sulfolobus acidocaldarius,* from the purification tanks."

"No mutations, or anything?"

"Not of any interest."

"You ought to teach them a few tricks."

Sloan smiled. "Oh, they can put on quite a show when the opportunity presents itself," he said placidly.

I knew what he was talking about. *Plexus* was practically run by microorganisms. Rotifers in the filtration ducts consumed other microbes that were harmful or toxic. Bacteria helped to repair the hull by excreting certain metals. Algae and azotobacter fixed nitrogen for the photosynthesis machines. Almost the entire *Plexus* cleaning system was based on microscopic organisms that quietly ate up grime and mold and bits of skin, scrubbed the air clean, processed sewage, and helped purify water.

Sloan was one of the people who took care of all these microbes. After two years of Rotation Placements, he had found his niche in Sustainable Services among other "Sussers" who monitored the health of our microscopic populations.

He called the populations his "little guys."

"Some of our *Halobacterium salinarum* are getting a bit frisky," Sloan said. "That's been interesting, because they're tough little guys. It's got to the point where adjusting pH levels just doesn't make an impression. We might have to do some genetic tweaking." His eyes narrowed, and another slow smile crept across his face. "It seems a pity to interfere, in a way, because I've always had a soft spot for the Darwinist position. Survival of the fittest and all that." Seeing my doubtful expression, he gave my arm a reassuring pat. "Don't worry, though. We have to guard against mutation in this environment."

Sloan could talk for hours about prokaryotic cells and *Mycoplasma genitalium* but only if given the chance. He was well aware that most people didn't share his enthusiasm for microbiology. "So tell me about the party," he said, abruptly changing course. "Was everyone there?"

"Pretty much everyone. Except Yestin. He was at MedLab."

"Ill?"

"Tests. Did you hear that Firminus threw the switch on us?" I asked, and Sloan blinked. We were sitting at his modest extension table, which was attached to the bulkhead. "He said he had to run some charts. Something's going on. My dad didn't make it home for supper."

"That's interesting," said Sloan.

"You haven't heard anything?"

Sloan shook his head. "Not a word."

"Dad was talking about an 'anomaly.'"

"Anomaly in what?"

"He didn't say."

Sloan rubbed his cheek thoughtfully. Then he shrugged. "Well," he said, "if it's anything important, we'll find out soon enough. So, what else can you tell me? What did Dygall do?"

Sloan always liked to hear about Dygall. He would lean back and absorb the news with an air of detached enjoyment. I had seen the same expression in his eyes whenever he and Dygall got together. You could have sworn that Sloan was observing the behavior of a particularly aggressive microbe.

I don't think Dygall liked him much.

"Dygall said we ought to expose ourselves to mimexic monsters," I reported. "Otherwise, our first alien encounter is going to scare us all to death."

Sloan raised an eyebrow.

"He also wants to run a Battle of Waterloo program for his next birthday," I added.

"Complete with mimexic monsters?"

"Maybe. I don't know. Caromy was there." I cleared my throat. Though I wanted to talk and talk about Caromy, I was also afraid of saying something stupid. "She was playing with the little kids," I added lamely.

"Oh?"

"She's very good with little kids."

"Yes." I got the impression, from Sloan's half smile, that he regarded such a talent as something to be expected in a person of only average intelligence. "So, was there any dancing?" he asked.

"A bit."

He nodded, and I decided to change the subject. I didn't feel like telling Sloan about my failure to dance with Caromy. It was getting too late. "Some of the music was pretty bad," I added, and we both smiled. "Plexus Mix, you know. Maybe Firminus could hear it on the Bridge. Maybe he threw the switch because he couldn't stand the noise."

"That wouldn't surprise me."

"Not that it was anywhere *near* as bad as the stuff I used to come up with," I had to concede.

"No." Sloan tapped his chin. "I seem to recall that yours had a somewhat cachinnating effect."

"A *what* effect?"

"Look it up," said Sloan with a glint in his eye. (I never left one of Sloan's Hobnobs without something to look up. He was relentless like that.) "So *Firminus* wanted to run those charts?"

"Yes."

"To check our course?"

"I suppose so."

He grunted. I watched him run the tip of his finger back and forth across his chin. "Maybe I'll give my father a call," he said at last. But when he tried, he couldn't get through. Firminus's comm-link wasn't cleared to receive.

The Bridge was busy.

Chapter Three

When the noise woke me up, I thought that Dad must have returned from the Bridge at long last. But I was wrong.

It was Mum, preparing to leave our cabin.

"What's going on?" I demanded groggily. I had climbed out of bed and crossed to the door of my room in about four shuffling steps. (It wasn't a very big room.) "Where are you going?"

"Oh dear." Mum was pulling on her shoes in the half-light. "I was trying to be quiet . . ."

"Is somebody sick?"

"No, my love. It's nothing like that."

"What, then?"

Mum hesitated, and that unnerved me. She wasn't normally the sort of person to pussyfoot around.

"It's not Dad, is it?" I asked in alarm.

"No, no! Tuddor's fine."

"Where is he? Isn't he back yet? What time is it?"

"About zero three." Mum rose from her seat. She hadn't combed her hair, I noticed. "Cheney, there's a Senate meeting on. I have to go. Your father, too."

I caught my breath. "A *Senate* meeting? *Now?*"

"I'm afraid so."

"But—but—" A Senate meeting at three o'clock in the morning could only be an emergency Senate meeting. And the only emergency Senate meeting ever before held on *Plexus* had occurred during the First Shift, some forty-three years previously.

On that occasion the ship had narrowly avoided a large meteor.

"Is it a meteor?" I gasped.

"No. It's something else."

"What?"

"I don't know. Please, Cheney, I'll tell you later. I have to go now. I'm sorry, my love. I wish I hadn't woken you." She crossed the room and kissed me on the forehead. "See if you can get back to sleep."

I couldn't, of course. How could I? An emergency Senate meeting had to mean that something bad was about to occur. So I sat in front of my Interface Array and logged on to our Core Artificial Intelligence Program, hoping that I might be able to dig up some information.

In those days CAIP was pretty accessible. The personnel files were heavily protected, but almost everything else was wide open—provided that you knew your way around. I did. I had to, because my Rotation Placement at the time was with Planning and Projection, the department that took care of CAIP and the Central Processing Unit or CPU. All of us "Capers" were required to have a thorough grasp of the programs that ran the ship. After two months at Planning and Projection, I had a good working knowledge of most of CAIP's functions, thanks to my supervisor, Arkwright. Arkwright knew CAIP more intimately than anyone else ever had.

Oddly enough, he wasn't a big fan. Although he agreed that CAIP was extraordinarily complex, he didn't regard it as a very "creative" program. It was, he said, too stable to be really interesting. Its designers had sacrificed flexibility for stability; CAIP, he maintained, was about as exciting as a condenser coil.

I suppose, after years of exposure to CAIP, he couldn't be blamed for getting a little bored. I disagreed with him, though. I was still coming to terms with the sheer extent and depth of that program. As for the CPU, it was a marvel. It had a self-assembly system based on hybridized DNA and a matrix like a neuron map. In other words, it wasn't the least bit boring to me. Neither was CAIP. Just because a program is accessible and user-friendly doesn't mean it's a great big yawn.

As accessible as CAIP was, however, I didn't have much luck with the Navigation data that night. My problem was that I still hadn't spent any time in Navigation. (My first Rotation Placement had been with Sustainable Services.) So a lot of the stuff that I riffled through didn't make much sense to me. Besides, I was tired. I wasn't thinking too clearly.

What I finally established was this: we were on a collision course with some kind of mysterious band of radiation. It was heading straight for us—a long drawn-out wave of energy hurtling through space at the speed of light. No one had worked out the exact composition of the wave or where it might have come from. No one had worked out whether we could dodge it.

I sat there with a strange feeling in the pit of my stomach. You see, there weren't any lifeboats on board *Plexus*. There were a couple of shuttle-pods, but each of them was big enough to hold only about twenty people, having been designed specifically for carrying the *Plexus* population, little by little, from the ship to any nearby habitable planet. They weren't equipped to support life for very long. They weren't big enough. Only *Plexus* was big enough.

It had been decided—long ago and far away—that lifeboats would be pointless. *Plexus* was our only chance of long-term survival in space. That's why we didn't have any lifeboats, or emergency beacons, or evacuation procedures. Why bother with things like that? There was no one out there to pick us up if we abandoned ship.

If *Plexus* died, we died.

Sitting in my room, I told myself that *Plexus* wouldn't die. It couldn't die. It had a multilayer pressure hull designed to repel every kind of radiation known to man. It had a coating of sol-gels (heat-resistant porous films). It was constructed out of nano-composite matter that contained atomic-force nanoprobes; they could repair faults on a subatomic level by enabling atoms to move back into low-energy positions. On top of that, the ship had a photocatalytic shield. I'm not exactly sure how this shield worked, but I do know that it responded to every frequency on the electromagnetic spectrum. The higher the frequency, the greater the response, which was a massive release of ions forming a kind of reflective barrier.

With all this at our disposal as well as our micrometeoroid deflector and backup thermal protection system, we couldn't be at risk. That's what I told myself. And despite a niggling sense of unease, I truly believed it. Somewhere deep down, in my very bones, I knew that *Plexus* wouldn't fail us.

Nevertheless, I was still awake when my parents finally returned at zero six, for a bite of breakfast and a word with me.

Mum took one look at my face and said, "You haven't slept a wink, have you?"

I shook my head.

"Oh, Cheney. You should have called. I'd have given you something."

"You were in a Senate meeting. I couldn't interrupt a Senate meeting."

"Yes, you could. You can call me anytime, you know that. Senate meeting or no Senate meeting."

"What's going on?" I could restrain myself no longer. "What's happening with the wave? Is it going to hit us?"

Dad peered at me. "You've been poking around in CAIP," he deduced.

"Yes, I have. But I don't understand . . ."

"Nobody understands." Dad turned to the food dispenser and jabbed at a few of the keys, frowning. (For some reason, he never quite mastered the food dispensers on *Plexus*.) "We don't know what we're dealing with, exactly. Not yet."

"Why?" I asked. "Didn't we get *anything* out of the probe?"

"Some early readings. That was before it passed through the wave. Since then, nothing. All we know is this isn't a type of cosmic emission that anyone's ever encountered before. Oh, damn—what have I done now?"

"You just canceled your order, Dad. Let me."

"Thanks." He stepped aside, and I keyed in his directives for him. Poor Dad had a bit of a problem with the physical world. He called himself "matter-incompatible."

"It's a bundle of contradictions, this wave," he continued as his pancakes appeared. "On the one hand, it's behaving rather like high-frequency radiation. On the other hand, it's a stream of subatomic particles that aren't quanta. Some of them aren't even identifiable as any of the three hundred or so types known to us already, though at least two of them appear to be elementary particles. It's very strange."

"But is it dangerous?" That's what *I* wanted to know. "Are we going to be all right?"

Dad glanced at Mum. "Oh, I'm sure we are," he said in the booming voice that always sounded so confident. "For all we know, the probe's just fine. The wave might be ahead of its signal, that's all."

"Anyway, your father's working on an alternative course," Mum added. "We might be able to outrun it. So to speak."

"But we'll have to hurry." Dad began to stuff down a pancake, using his fingers. "Seems to be subject to random surge variations . . . which makes it hard to plot, of course."

"We're on yellow alert," Mum interrupted. "That's the important thing."

"Yellow alert?" I was dazed. "What does that mean?"

"Oh, Cheney." Mum sounded disappointed. We were all supposed to know our alert drills by heart. I tried to concentrate.

"He hasn't slept," Dad mumbled through a mouthful of pancake. "Maybe you should give him something to calm him down."

"I'm fine. Really." I'd remembered by then. Yellow alert. Of course. "Pressure suits and scheduled stations. Stand by to brace," I recited.

"Correct," said Dad.

"But I don't *have* a scheduled station," I pointed out. Capers had no specific site allocations—they could work out of their cabins, if they wanted to—and anyway, I was supposed to be sticking with Arkwright. "Where's Arkwright going to be?"

"On the Bridge," Dad replied. "I'll take you."

He and Mum exchanged another glance. Then Mum hustled me into my pressure suit, which was a transparent, plasma-film thing with a built-in thermionic cooler system and an emergency oxygen supply pump. Happily I didn't have to seal the hood. Not for a yellow alert. Even the glove assemblies were optional.

Dad needed a lot of help getting into his.

"It's sticking to me," he complained.

"It is not," Mum retorted. "It just feels like that."

"It's too small for me, Comet, I swear."

"Nonsense."

They ended up in fits of nervous giggles because he completely messed up the boot assembly attachment. My father could break *anything,* given half a chance. He was brilliant, but he was clumsy—always knocking over cups and running into bulkheads. He had oversized feet, and a huge voice, and one of those big, loose-jointed bodies that are terribly uncoordinated, no matter how much training they're put through.

He was also a good bit older than Mum, so that can't have helped his agility rating. His long wispy curls were quite gray by then; his face was pouchy and his movements were slow. But that was all right, he used to say. My mother had enough energy for both of them.

I suppose I took after Mum in the looks department. I wasn't especially big or especially loud. Nor was I especially clumsy. I had her pale eyes and skin, and my hair, though thicker, was a similar brown to hers. But when it came to energy levels, I was much more like Dad.

The two of us working together couldn't accomplish half as much as Mum could. Not unless the work involved particle physics or something.

"How long have we got?" I asked them. "I mean—when are we supposed to be hitting this thing?"

"If we hit it at all," Mum corrected, and Dad said, "We've got a few hours yet. When we've finished our calculations, we'll know the exact time." He accepted a spare glucose bar from Mum and tucked it into his pocket. "My guess is about eleven-hundred."

"Have you eaten, Cheney?"

"Yes," I replied—although I knew that, in my mother's opinion, one dry biscuit from the bottom of a drawer wasn't a proper meal. The trouble was I didn't feel hungry. "When do we go into red alert, then?"

"When the time is right," said Dad.

Mum squeezed my arm. "I'll be along, Cheney," she murmured. "Everything's been arranged. My emergency station is on the Bridge with you and Tuddor. There's no need to worry."

No need to worry. That's what all the Shifters were told. And it's what we believed. What was the point of panicking? It wouldn't do any good. Besides, our world had always been so stable. We could hardly comprehend anything else, especially when our parents remained reassuringly calm. Mum was calm. Dad was calm. (Slightly distracted but calm.) Out in the tube there weren't any disturbances. A few people were walking around in their pressure suits, and even they were perfectly calm—though perhaps a little preoccupied. Everything else seemed normal.

When the next OTV arrived at our junction, Sloan was inside. He, too, was calm. In fact, he appeared more concerned about his "little guys" than he was about anything else. As we sat there behind Dad and one of the Tekkies from Technical Fault Protection, Sloan muttered something to me about the effects of high-frequency radiation on various bacteria colonies that hadn't been developed "with intensive exposure in mind."

"Anything much over seven hundred and fifty terahertz and they're sizzled," he said. "Of course, they're nowhere near the hull, but still . . ."

"Aren't you more worried about us?" I asked him quietly. And he shrugged.

"No," he said. "Not really."

"Why not?"

"Because Firminus isn't." Sloan crossed his legs, leaning back in his seat. "Firminus doesn't think we're going to be too badly affected. This ship is built like a fort."

"All the same, it might be hard. Just getting through the next few hours, I mean."

Sloan smiled. He fixed me with an odd look—lazy but intent. Then he leaned over.

"You won't feel a thing," he murmured.

"What?"

"MedLab has it all under control." As I stared at him in total confusion, he went on to explain. "Any red alert means that they adulterate the air supply. Automatically. *Before* you seal your pressure suit. Procedure M34a."

"Huh?"

"It means that no one's going to panic. Won't be able to. We'll all be under a form of sedation." Watching me, Sloan added, "It's the logical thing to do. We'll be put down, too, if it gets to the point of hull disintegration. Didn't you know? There's some kind of painless neurotoxin release in our ID band—"

"There is not!" I pulled away in horror.

Dad turned around. "What's wrong?" he asked.

"Sloan says—"

"It's all right," Sloan interrupted. "I was teasing. Sorry. It's neither the time nor the place."

For a moment Dad studied him. Then he studied me. Then he grunted and returned to his conversation with the Tekkie.

"We're not supposed to know about M34a," Sloan whispered, putting his mouth to my ear. "It's part of the security protocol. Very hush-hush."

"Then why do *you* know?" I demanded softly.

"Because my mother spilled the beans." Sloan smiled again. "She has such a big mouth."

((35))

I was shocked. It seemed to me that Sadira had been pretty irresponsible. My mother was the *head* of MedLab, and she'd never told *me* about Procedure M34a. I was about to say something, but we arrived at Navigation and I had to get out. Dad got out, too, though not before addressing a few words to Sloan.

"If there's a red alert," said Dad, "you come straight back here."

Sloan nodded carelessly.

"I mean it," Dad insisted. "Your mother will be here, and so will Firminus."

"He told me."

"It was all worked out a long time ago, Sloan," my father added. He sounded very serious all of a sudden. His voice rumbled in his chest, deep and strong. "The day you were born, in fact. There's only one place for you during a red alert. Is that clear?"

Another nod from Sloan—not so careless this time. The hatch shut. Then the OTV slid away, leaving Dad and me standing on the platform.

We arrived on the Bridge just after zero seven-forty.

Chapter Four

When I was very small, I didn't understand why the Bridge was called "the Bridge." I knew about bridges—there was one at the Depot, connecting two gangways—and the large white compartment on A deck didn't resemble one at all. Only later, after studying Earth history for a while, did I begin to understand. A bridge was originally a narrow, elevated platform from which the captain of a sailing ship issued orders and surveyed the horizon. Even when this platform became an enclosed room and the captain's orders were transmitted rather than shouted, the word "bridge" still remained.

On board *Plexus* we didn't have a captain. Nor did we have any windows. (With artificial gravity in place, windows weren't really an option.) But we did have a Navigation department, and that department was centered around the Bridge.

The Bridge was a highly specialized location. It contained an outstanding Interface Array, which included special functions available nowhere else. The Mimexis Chamber was also attached to the Bridge. Like the Depot and the pump stations, the Bridge was one of the few places on *Plexus* rated "First Level." This meant that the door wouldn't open automatically for every person who approached it. Your DNA signature had to be cleared by a scanner if you wanted to get in. Either that or you had to be with someone who had First Level clearance.

My father had First Level clearance. That's why I was admitted. Upon entering the Bridge compartment that fateful morning, I saw that it was bursting at the seams. Every chair was filled. There must have been two dozen people in the room. Arkwright was there poring over a screen. So were Merrit and Firminus.

Merrit lifted her hand to me.

"Hello, Cheney!" said Haido, who was one of the Navvies, like Dad. A round-faced woman with crisp gray curls worn close to her head, Haido doted on all the Shifters. Even at such a tense time she seemed happy to see me. "Have you come to help your dad today?" she asked, flashing her dimples.

"Uh—no." I gestured at Arkwright. "I'm with him."

"Oh. Yes, of course. You're in Planning and Projection now, aren't you? Lucky old boiler, she doesn't deserve it."

Haido was referring to the Central Processing Unit. She was the only person I ever knew who talked about the CPU as if it were a person—a little old lady, to be precise. "Granny's got indigestion this morning," Haido would say. Or, "That mean old bag ate up my selection criteria!"

She was nice, though, was Haido. Very nice and very smart.

"Off you go, then," she said. "Better not keep Arky waiting. We're a bit busy today."

As if I didn't know! Firminus, in particular, was a wreck, all hollow cheeks and red-rimmed eyes. He was hovering over one of the other Navvies, his gaze fixed on a cascade of twinkling numbers. Beside him, Arkwright was playing CAIP like a musical instrument, his long bony fingers moving smoothly from pad to pad, node to node. I had to tap him twice on the shoulder before he noticed me.

"Oh! Cheney!"

"What should I do?"

"Umm . . ." Arkwright blinked. With his huge bulbous eyes, pointed chin, and long neck he looked like a particular species of insect that evolved on Earth; I can't remember its name, but it used to carry its front legs in a curious position, elbows crooked, wrists pressed together. You often saw Arkwright in the same kind of pose as he sat hunched at his Array. "Shouldn't you be with your mother?" he asked, and I flushed. It wasn't as if I were a kid anymore.

"She's coming," I muttered. "She'll be here if we go on red alert."

"Ah."

"What should I do in the meantime?" I glanced at his Array. "What are those? Probability projections?"

Arkwright didn't answer. He looked around. "Is there a chair?" he queried.

"I'll find one. I'll get one from across the street."

"All right, then. You can set up here, next to me."

((39))

"And do what?"

"Cumulative frequency sampling."

So that was what I did for the next couple of hours: cumulative frequency sampling. There was a subprogram you could run that . . . Oh, I won't go into it now. What's the point? I'll just say that Lais Ulrich—who was on Arkwright's team—had been put in charge of endless probability calculations, relating to possible outcomes of radiation impact. There was a lot of data to manage, and my job was to sift through all this stuff about the effects of primary cosmic rays on fullerenol polyimides in the hull, and so forth.

I don't know if it was vital work or not. It certainly wasn't much fun. Lais probably could have handled it herself, along with everything else that she was juggling, because she had an amazing triple-track mind. Despite her nervous disposition she was incredibly efficient; I had seen her perform a number of complex operations *while talking about someone's blood tests.* (She was a chronic gossip, on top of everything else.)

That morning, however, even Lais was quiet. It was strange to see her curled up at her Array like Arkwright, glum and silent and attentive. She didn't even ask me about Haemon's party. She just nodded at me, once; after that we communicated solely through CAIP. I transmitted my data to her, and she channeled it through to Sustainable Services, or Technical Fault Protection, or whatever other department required information updates.

Though we never once opened our mouths, we still had plenty to say.

About twenty minutes after I arrived, Dad came up with a final trajectory for the emission wave. This meant that Firminus had to calculate a change of course—for the first time in forty-three years. He then had to initiate a burn: the longest burn in *Plexus* history. He had to ignite the engine and keep it burning for all of ten seconds.

No wonder he looked like death warmed over.

Thinking back now, I realize how momentous that burn actually was. For the first time my whole world was shifting on its axis. All my life I'd been traveling in one direction, at a constant speed. Now that was about to change. Yet as Firminus barked orders and the status reports rolled in, I couldn't quite grasp the full import of what was happening. I had a job to do, after all. I had data to process. And everyone around me was busily working away in an atmosphere of total concentration. Is it any wonder that I took my cue from the adults and failed to give this unprecedented event the appreciation that was due to it?

When we were finally told to brace, I didn't even shut my eyes for the countdown.

Not that there was the slightest cause for concern. Firminus knew exactly what he was doing. He had a firm grip on every aspect of the maneuver: the Trajectory Orientation Sensors, the Reaction Control System, the Rotation Stabilizers . . . absolutely everything. The thrust, when it came, was hardly noticeable— just a slight shudder. There was no power-drain. No obvious gravimetric problems.

After a few taut seconds everyone broke into applause.

"There's nothing to celebrate," said Firminus dryly. "Not yet."

((41))

And he was right, of course. Because despite the burn—despite four thousand two hundred and twenty-five kilonewtons of thrust and a perfectly calibrated trajectory shift—we had no chance of reaching the speed of light. We had no chance of outstripping that emission wave. All we had achieved with our burn was to change our point of impact. Instead of hitting the center of the stream we would be grazing its weaker, narrower, outer limits.

That, at least, is what Merrit told me.

We met up at the food dispenser and exchanged a few quiet words. This was at zero nine-fifteen. I noticed that her hairstyle was a lot less elaborate than usual. I also noticed the slightly bewildered look in her eyes.

"Hi," she said.

"Hi."

"Lemonade?"

"Please."

"*I'm* having one, too."

But when she tried to order herself a lemonade, CAIP wouldn't dispense it. She had already used up her entire weekly quota.

"Oh, for heaven's sake!" she growled. "You'd think on today of all days . . . !"

"Here," I said. "Have mine."

"What?" She glanced over her shoulder, but no one was paying us any attention. "Well . . . all right. Thanks," she murmured. "Much obliged."

"How's it going?"

"Okay. I guess." She watched me order an orange juice. "Tuddor's amazing."

"Yeah."

"He doesn't seem too worried," she said, and we exchanged a long glance over the rims of our cups.

"It'll be all right," I told her at last. "We still might outrun this thing."

"No." She shook her head.

"Are you sure? Because—"

"I'm sure. So are they." She jerked her thumb at the rest of the Navvies. "We're nowhere near outrunning it. All we can do is nick one of the edges where the stream isn't as thick or as strong."

"Oh." That was bad news. "So there *will* be a red alert?"

"For sure. Won't be long now." Merrit hesitated. "I've got to leave before then," she added. "My parents will both be in Technical Fault Protection. At the Depot. They want me back in TFP with them."

"Of course." I drained my cup and returned it to the dispenser. "My mum's the same. She'll be joining us here."

"So, if I don't get another chance, Cheney . . ." She put down her own cup before presenting me with a shy and hesitant smile. "Take care."

She didn't say goodbye. Hardly anyone ever said goodbye on *Plexus*. Why bother? We had nowhere else to go. Yet as I watched Merrit return briskly to her station, it dawned on me that maybe I *should* have said goodbye. Theoretically we might be facing the end of everything. The end of the *human race,* even. We had long ago lost contact with Earth; what if life on that planet was finally extinct? It was unlikely but not impossible.

Even at this point, however, I had no real sense of impending

((43))

doom. My heart refused to accept what my mind was telling it. We had survived the burn, and that had been a historic turning point. It seemed natural to assume that we would also survive the emission wave.

Nevertheless, my thoughts fixed on Caromy. It occurred to me that this would be the perfect time to tell her how I felt. At last I had a good excuse; how could she blame me for speaking out when we were facing the greatest peril of our lives? She wouldn't, I felt sure.

No one really needed me on the Bridge. I knew that. All the same, I asked Arkwright for permission to go to the toilet, which was located in a cubicle just inside the door. Arkwright nodded. (I don't think he even heard.) Dad threw me an inquiring look but seemed satisfied when I mouthed "toilet." I slipped away without attracting any other kind of attention.

Once in the cubicle, however, I sat for a moment. My sense of responsibility had suddenly ambushed me; I knew that, before communicating with Caromy, I should do the right thing and call some other people. Dygall, for instance, who was my Little Brother. Yestin, my fellow Shifter. I had a duty to these people, I realized. They had to know that I was watching out for them.

So I patched through to Dygall, who was with his parents in the food processing area.

"Cheney?" he said. "What's up?"

"How are things with you, Dygall?"

"Oh, I'm having a great time." Dygall spoke sarcastically. "We're all just sitting around, twiddling our thumbs. It's real exciting."

"Don't you think we've had enough excitement for one day?"

"*You* might have. You're on the Bridge, aren't you? I hope they know what they're doing up there."

"Of course they do. Don't worry."

"Can't they dodge this thing?"

"No. It's too fast. And too big."

"I wish I was with you. No one knows anything around here."

"You stay with your parents, Dygall."

"If my father tries to counsel me, I'll break his teeth."

"Don't say that. It's not funny."

"He's got us playing games, Cheney."

"Well—that sounds like fun."

"I tell you, if it keeps on like this, we'll all be *happy* to die. Just to escape from his riddles."

I had to laugh. I couldn't help it. "Dygall, we're not going to die," I said. "The chances are so slim. Really. Come on, now— you're always complaining about how bored you are. Isn't this exciting enough for you?"

"It would be more exciting on the Bridge."

"Just call me," I told him. "If you need me, just call."

I finally managed to sign off. Then I called Yestin, who didn't seem terribly interested in the yellow alert. He kept talking about his Robo-dog, which he had named Bam. Bam still had a glitch in his circuits—something about electron flows. We discussed that for a while. Then I asked Yestin if the burn had affected him in any way; I knew that he would be sensitive to the slightest change in our gravitational forces.

"Oh—I was feeling a bit sick," Yestin admitted.

((45))

"Really? That's tough. I'm sorry."

"Hey, it's no big deal. I'm always sick. Anyway, I feel fine now. Mum gave me something." The Robo-dog barked. "You know, he doesn't jump so well. I think I'll put springs in his legs."

"Where are you, anyway?"

"GeoLab. With Dad."

"And your mother?"

"She's here, too."

"Well, that's good. So you're all right, then."

"Yeah, I'm okay. I guess. Thanks for asking."

"Take care, Yestin."

"Cheney!"

"What?"

A pause. At last Yestin said, "It's weird, isn't it?"

"What?"

"All this. The alert and everything."

"Oh. Yeah. It's certainly unusual." I tried to sound positive, and it wasn't so hard. "But we're going to be fine. Don't worry."

"I won't."

"Look after yourself."

"You, too."

"Linkdown."

My heart was in my mouth when I called Caromy. You won't believe this, but the prospect of talking to her frightened me more than the emission wave did. I had to clear my throat several times before patching through.

She seemed surprised to hear my voice.

"Cheney? Where are you?" she said.

"The Bridge. Where are you?"

"Pump station one, of course. What's the matter?"

"Well . . ." I took a deep breath. "You see . . . I just . . ."

"It'll be all right, honey. You'll see."

"Yes, I know. But—I mean, if it *isn't*—"

"It will." She spoke firmly. "I know this crew. I trust this crew. This crew will get us through, and so will *Plexus*."

It could have been me talking. Caromy was doing her duty as a Big Sister to every Shifter on board. But that's not what I wanted.

"Caromy, that's not why I called you." I suddenly thought: *Why didn't I do this on Vindow? I need to see her face!* "Can we switch to Vindow, Caromy?"

"Oh, Cheney, it's not a good time. I'm inputting right now. What did you want to say? Is that naughty Dygall bothering you again?"

"No, no. It's nothing like that."

"What, then?"

I cleared my throat. "If something bad happens—"

"It won't."

"But if it *does*, Caromy! If it does, just in case, I wanted to tell you . . ." What? I tried to find the words. "You're an inspiration!" I blurted out. "To all of us! Especially me."

"Oh, Cheney. That's so sweet. But you're pretty inspirational yourself, you know. All the little kids look up to you; I know they do. You're a great role model. You're always so kind and thoughtful, and you never lose your temper, or forget about our ultimate goals—"

((47))

"No, no!" She had misunderstood. I wasn't talking about the Brotherhood program. I wasn't talking about civic duty. "That's not the point! What I want to say is this . . ."

But I never did say it. Because at that moment *Plexus* was put on red alert.

And Caromy had to sign off.

Chapter Five

Things started to happen very quickly. After I left the cubicle, I discovered that my portable chair was no longer considered safe. Instead, Haido had yanked open a series of emergency hatches in the floor, out of which had sprung five extra chairs. One of these was given to me. It didn't automatically adapt itself to my contours like the other seats in the compartment, but it was fitted with straps and buckles and wouldn't slide around if we faced a bumpy ride.

Unfortunately my new seat was nowhere near an Array. So I had to sit doing nothing while all around me the Bridge buzzed with activity.

Estimated time of impact was in exactly one hour. Before then every loose article had to be packed away or strapped down. Every emergency procedure had to be checked and rechecked. Every person on board had to report to his or her emergency station, wherever that might be.

Within minutes the Bridge was flooded with new arrivals. Before they appeared, however, Merrit left. She passed me on her way out, but she couldn't stop. She didn't have time.

Our eyes met, and then she was gone.

Rarely had I ever heard the Public Address System used. I gasped at the sound of that cool, female voice:

Attention. This is a red alert. Please lockdown and brace. All crew, stand by for impact.

I felt as if CAIP itself was speaking to me.

My mother arrived with Sloan and Sadira. The moment I saw them, I immediately felt better—and then wondered if the happy gas might be to blame. Could it have kicked in already? When Sloan seated himself next to me, on one of the foldout chairs, I asked him for his opinion.

"It's possible," he said with a shrug.

"I don't feel as scared as I thought I would. Do you?"

Sloan smiled, his inky gaze roaming the compartment. "Nothing to be scared of," he replied.

"I called Dygall. And Yestin. To make sure they were all right."

"Well done."

"Caromy, too. She was *really* calm."

A grunt.

"Merrit's gone to Technical Fault Protection. She says we're going to graze the edge of this thing." Sloan's smile broadened until I could actually see his teeth. "What is it?" I demanded. "What's so funny?"

"I think the happy gas might have kicked in," he murmured.

"Huh?"

"You don't usually talk this much."

That shut me up. I watched my mother circle the compartment, distributing pills. They were supposed to counteract the effects of gravity reduction: the fluid loss, the nausea, the congested sinuses. She was also telling everyone to seal their pressure suits. As she made each stop, I tried to distract myself by putting names to the faces around me. Conal, the brusque little Navvy with the big nose and fluffy hair, played some kind of instrument. A viola, was it? He played in a quartet with Sloan's supervisor, Ottilie, from BioLab. Landry was a champion basketball player, and had been part of the team that discovered the graviton back on Earth. Lais had been granted breeding privileges for the following year. But there were others about whom I knew nothing.

Counting heads, I realized that there were twenty-one of us on the Bridge. Would I be dying with these twenty other people?

My response to this question was so calm that I knew at once: the happy gas *must* have kicked in.

"All right, boys, I want you to take these," Mum announced, dropping a tiny pill into my hand and another into Sloan's. "Then I want those glove assemblies on, and I'll tell you when to seal up."

"I didn't call Haemon."

"What's that, honey?"

"I should have called Haemon," I fretted. "Haemon gets so worried about things, but he won't ask questions. And Inaret. Inaret likes me."

((51))

Mum patted my cheek. "It's all right," she said. "It'll be all right."

"Where are you sitting?"

"Here. Right here beside you." Mum turned to Sloan. "Sloan, would you mind moving down one? Tuddor wants to sit in that seat."

Sloan looked at her for a moment. "Sure," he said softly.

"Your mother will be in the next seat. On the end."

So there was a bit of a reshuffle as my mother explored her own chair, looking for somewhere safe to put her Medkit. She finally stuffed it behind a snap-lock hatch under the armrest.

Attention. This is a red alert. Please lockdown and brace. All crew, stand by for impact.

"I wish they wouldn't keep saying that," Sadira complained, securing her own Medkit. "It just makes everyone nervous."

Sloan caught my eye and winked.

"Can we have a drink before we seal up?" I asked my mother.

"All right. Be quick, though."

"I bet everyone could do with a shot of brandy," Sadira remarked, and I wondered how she was going to fit all that rippling, bouncy black hair into her headpiece. It astonished me that she hadn't already pinned it up—though when I gave it some thought, I realized that I never *had* seen Sadira's hair pinned up. Ever. "Failing that," she went on, "perhaps a good, strong coffee."

"Ha-ha," said my mother. "Richsip *only*, please, Cheney. It's the best thing."

"All right." Richsip, the fortified water that we were supposed to drink most of the time, wasn't exactly my favorite. But I did what I was told. It never even crossed my mind that for my last-ever drink I deserved something tasty.

I suppose the happy gas was blocking out thoughts of that kind.

Hovering at the food dispenser, watching my dad peering at a subatomic model from every possible angle, I wasn't thinking about how much I loved him. I was wondering if the construct in front of him was an antihydrogen atom: were those positrons orbiting antiprotons? I couldn't tell. I didn't know enough. I didn't understand the color coding.

Merrit would have known, I felt sure. She was so brilliant.

Attention. This is a red alert. Please lockdown and brace. All crew prepare for impact in E minus fifteen minutes.

Fifteen minutes! That gave me a shock. Where on earth had the time gone?

My father raised his head suddenly. "Lockdown," he ordered just as Firminus said the same thing, "Lockdown!"

Dad began to pace around the room scanning the Array. He stopped behind Arkwright and squeezed his shoulder.

"Locking down periphery circuits," said Arkwright. "And . . . conversion clamps."

"Lockdown on Photovoltaic Arrays," Haido announced.

"Confirmation through from TFP," said Lais. "Lockdown on all remote access systems. Lockdown on alpha rotary joint."

"Lockdown on docking bay."

The noise level rose. Mum beckoned to me. "Come here," she said. When I reached her, she jerked my mask over my face and sealed it. "Cheney seven oh four linkup." I could see her mouthing the words before her code beeped on my voice patch. I gave her a clear-to-receive.

"How does that feel?" she asked. It was odd; her question came through my transmitter just a fraction after she uttered it, like an echo of the faint, muffled noise that I could still hear through the insulation of my headpiece. The effect was disconcerting.

"Okay," I replied. It had always surprised me during our safety drills that I didn't feel suffocated inside my pressure suit. This time, I was surprised all over again. The cooling system worked wonderfully. "It feels fine."

"Tell me if you think something's wrong."

Sloan, meanwhile, was dragging on his glove assemblies. I buckled myself in, then followed suit. Sadira collapsed onto a chair. She twisted her hair up, spearing it with a single clip, as the lockdown reports continued. My mother did a last circuit of the compartment, reminding people to seal their suits, before returning to her own seat. A series of checks followed: multispectral scanners—check; Pho-Cat sensors—check; Orbital Maneuvering System—check. Over where Firminus stood, a sudden flurry of activity followed his command to lockdown engines. My stomach seemed to lift and roll, before settling again.

Because they were shouting across the room, I could hear the crew's voices quite clearly, even through my headpiece.

"And . . . terminate!"

"Lockdown on fuel cells!"

"Lockdown on vents, here!"

Mum leaned toward me. "Do you feel sick?" she asked through the Audio Interlink Network.

"No," I replied.

"Tell me if you feel sick."

Attention. This is a red alert. Please lockdown and brace. All crew prepare for impact in E minus ten minutes.

Dad was discussing something with Firminus. They stood, heads together, while around them their teams tightened straps and adjusted pressure seals. Lais was calling someone; I could tell by the way she murmured into her collar. Landry suddenly bolted into the toilet cubicle. Mum yelled across to Arkwright.

"Arkwright! Please seal up; you know the drill!"

And then the room became quiet, as most of the activity ceased. Various people were monitoring the close-range sensor input. My father was running an analysis. As for Arkwright, he was still deep in the bowels of CAIP, for some reason.

But the rest of us were suddenly left with time on our hands—Firminus included. I couldn't believe what he did next. Moving even more stiffly than usual, he crossed the room until he reached his wife. Then he bent and kissed her on the mouth.

I don't know if I'd really thought much about Firminus until that moment. To me he was simply Sloan's father—and not nearly as good a father as my own dad. Firminus had always seemed hard and quiet and unapproachable. I couldn't imagine ever coming to him with a problem. I couldn't imagine how Sloan had endured that rigid, implacable control while he was growing up.

Yet there on the Bridge I suddenly saw how much Firminus loved his family, and was reassured.

Whether he kissed Sloan as well, I'm not certain. Because I looked away at that point. But I do know that Firminus returned to his own seat shortly afterward and slowly, methodically strapped himself in. He was pulling his mask down when my mother dropped into the chair beside me.

"Tuddor," she said. (I could tell by the way her mouth moved.)

Dad looked around. I'd never seen him so puffy around the eyes before. He nodded, then stooped to exchange a few words with Haido. She inclined her head. He straightened. Slowly he surveyed the room. Sadira's hair was now concealed by her headpiece. Landry was returning from the toilet cubicle. Arkwright was struggling with his pressure seal.

Dad cracked a smile.

"You people look like a double order of individually wrapped glucose bars," he boomed, and there was a ripple of nervous, muted laughter. At least I think there was. I could see shoulders shaking and mouths stretching.

Attention. This is a red alert. Please lockdown and brace. All crew prepare for impact in E minus five minutes.

Mum helped my father to seal up, after which he sat down beside me. To my amazement, he managed the straps all by himself. My voice patch beeped. I gave a clear-to-receive before I realized who was calling.

"Cheney?"

"Dygall?"

"What's happening?"

"Five minutes to impact, Dygall, haven't you heard?"

"Yes, I know *that*. I mean, what's everyone doing up there?"

"Waiting. What do you think?"

"Hasn't somebody had a brilliant, last-minute idea?"

"No."

"Hmm. Pity."

"Is there something I can do for you, Dygall?"

A pause.

"No," he said. Then: "See ya." And he signed off.

Attention. This is a red alert. Please lockdown and brace. All crew prepare for impact in E minus three minutes.

"Tuddor twelve linkup," I said, and when the channel was open, asked, "Dad? What does E mean?"

"Hmm?"

"I said, what does E mean?"

"It means event. As in 'event minus three minutes.'" Hearing my mother's signal code, Dad accepted her transmission. "What's up, Comet?"

"I hope Yestin's all right," my mother remarked. "I just know the rotation stabilizers were affected during that burn."

"Poor Lais," Dad murmured. I could see why. Lais was bent forward, staring at her knees. Mum took my hand and squeezed it. She didn't let go.

. . . Prepare for impact in E minus two minutes.

Dad put his arm around my shoulders. It felt so heavy. Mum said, "I love you, Cheney." That's when the happy gas stopped working so well. My eyes felt hot, and I blinked.

"Rats," said Dad, his voice rumbling low through his transmitter. "I forgot to put my laundry in the dump."

That made me giggle. I suppose it was meant to. I had the weirdest giggling fit, for some reason.

Prepare for impact in E minus sixty seconds.

"Now, has everyone gone to the toilet?" Dad went on.

"Da-ad!" I protested. "Please!"

"Comet, what happens if we fart inside these things? Is there some kind of venting mechanism?"

"Da-ad!"

"What?"

"How can you be so *stupid*?"

"Oh, it's not easy. Not for a man of my intellect. But I've been in training."

Prepare for impact in E minus thirty seconds.

Mum applied more pressure to my hand. Dad's arm tightened around my shoulders. Then he tickled me.

"Ow! Stop it!"

"What? I'm not doing anything."

"Yes, you are." I knew what it was, too. "Don't worry, Dad. I'm okay." I wasn't, of course. There were tears in my eyes. "I love you, Dad."

. . . in E minus ten seconds.

I saw Dad reach across me with his free hand.

. . . nine . . .

Mum's free hand met his.

. . . eight . . .

There was dead silence.

. . . seven . . .

Suddenly I found myself praying. I don't know why. It's not as if any all-powerful force governing the universe—if it existed—was going to pay the slightest bit of attention to me. But I prayed anyway.

. . . six . . .

Please, I prayed, *let us survive this thing.*

... five ...

"Cheney," said Dad, "you are my greatest achievement."

... four ...

I closed my eyes.

... three ...

I caught my breath.

... two ...

I thought: This can't be happening.

... one ...

Chapter Six

The encounter lasted nine seconds.

We sat there, and nothing much happened. No alarms went off. No vibrations shook the hull. The lights didn't flicker. The temperature remained stable.

Then Firminus, who had been watching his Array, transmitted a general announcement over the Audio Interlink Network: "Event cessation. Mark: eleven-hundred zero two." He turned in his seat to look at my father.

"Are you sure?" asked Dad, forgetting that he was still sharing a signal link with me and Mum. For that reason, I heard his exchange with Firminus quite clearly.

"CAIP is sure," said Firminus.

"Arkwright oh five linkup," said Dad. "Arkwright? What's your take?"

"It's all negative readings, Tuddor," Arkwright replied. "We're through."

"Let me see," Dad said, and unstrapped himself.

"Tuddor!" Mum exclaimed sharply.

"It's all right, Quenby. We're clear." Dad went over to Arkwright's Array. Arkwright turned to Lais, and said something that I couldn't hear, because he was using a different signal link. Lais nodded. Dad suddenly broke his connection with me; perhaps he didn't want any distractions.

I turned to my mum.

"Are—are we through?" I stammered.

"I think so."

"Is it still a red alert?"

"Technically. Until all the reports come in." Mum unbuckled her harness. "Speaking of which, I'd better run some Med-scans."

Suddenly everyone seemed to be moving. I looked around, bewildered. Had we done it, then? Had we made it through? My heart was still hammering away.

Sloan, I noticed, was heading for the door. But he stopped before reaching it. He turned to face his father.

They were conversing into their voice patches. Firminus probably wanted to know where Sloan thought he was going. Sloan probably replied that he was on his way to the BioLab, to check on his "little guys."

Firminus, however, prevented him, and Sloan returned quietly to his seat. He didn't even look in my direction.

Sadira had already crossed to one of the Arrays; I'm not sure whether she had seen her son's attempted departure or not. Probably not. Landry was making for the toilet again, and I wondered why. Arkwright unsealed his headpiece, pushing back the mask.

"Arkwright!" said Mum.

"Atmospheric readings are through, Quenby." I was picking up Arkwright on my mother's signal link. I don't think he knew that I was connected. "They're absolutely normal."

"So far, maybe. Arkwright, we're still on red alert—"

"Well, all right." Arkwright swung around to face her, wearing that attentive yet utterly detached expression I knew so well from our training sessions together. "You tell me. Atmospherics are normal. Temperature's normal. Gravity's normal. We're not braced for impact. You're the Chief Medic—it's your call. Shall we cancel the seal or not?"

Mum hesitated. She glanced at Sadira, who was peering at vital-sign readouts from all over the ship. Then Mum began to ask her about pulmonary alerts and oxyhemoglobin levels, and I cut our signal link. I didn't feel that I could cope with medical jargon. Not right then.

Almost immediately my voice patch beeped. I recognized the signal code as Merrit's.

Naturally I gave her a clear-to-receive.

"Merrit?"

"Cheney?"

"What's wrong?"

"Nothing. I mean—what's happening? Are we through?"

"Yes."

"Really?"

"Really. Is there any damage at your end?"

"I don't know. I don't think so." A pause. "Wait up. I'll get back to you. There's a lot going on down here."

And she signed off. Meanwhile, Mum had given the all clear.

We could unseal our pressure suits. From one end of the Bridge to the other, masks were being pulled off.

As always, I smelled the air when I first broke my seal—just for a few seconds. After that, I got used to it again and stopped noticing its slightly burned, electrical odor.

"TFP's picking up microscopic energy surges around the hull," Lais was saying. "Practically on a pico level."

"Let me look," said Arkwright.

"They're not quite sure what it means," Lais went on.

Arkwright grunted. Dad approached him and peered over his shoulder intently.

Sadira said, "Uh-oh." She pointed at her Array. "Quenby? Check that out."

"Damn it," my mother said, then looked around. She seemed startled. "Where is he?"

Sadira also scanned the room, her brow puckered. "I don't know . . ."

"Sloan? Have you seen Landry?"

Sloan blinked.

"He's in the toilet," I observed.

Sadira sprang to her feet. Mum said, "*Damn* it!" again. They both headed for the toilet cubicle; then Mum stopped and added, "I'll get the Medkit."

"What's wrong?" I asked.

But the question didn't need answering. By that time Sadira had reached the cubicle door and pulled it open. Landry was slumped on the floor inside.

Sloan jumped to his feet while I fumbled with my harness.

"Quenby?" Now Dad had noticed. "What the hell—?"

"It's okay," said Mum. "Don't worry."

"What happened?"

"Look, Quenby. He's hit his head," Sadira announced. She was squatting beside Landry, supporting him. He seemed only half awake.

There was blood on his temple.

"Shock," said my mother, yanking her Medkit from the hatch where she'd stowed it. "He must have been feeling faint—"

"He's been vomiting," Sadira remarked with a wince. "There should have been an alarm."

"There probably was. We just missed it in all the fuss." Mum pushed her Medkit across the floor to Sadira. "It's all right, Tuddor. We'll get him checked out. Sadira will take him to MedLab."

"It's not some kind of radiation sickness, is it?" Sloan asked quietly before anyone else could. A good half of the Bridge crew had paused in their work, anxious to find out what had happened. Arkwright and Firminus didn't appear to have registered the disturbance. They were still squinting at readouts.

Mum shook her head.

"It's fluid loss," she replied, "on top of nervous shock and the effects of—I mean, he's had a bad reaction. To a drug." Her sudden embarrassment made me wonder if the drug in question might have been happy gas. "It's a combination of things, but none of them is cause for general concern."

"Are you sure?" asked Dad. He spoke levelly. "I want to be sure, Comet."

"We'll check him out," my mother promised. "We'll give him a thorough scan; don't worry. There's no evidence of cellular breakdown at this point."

"So, am I cleared to go?" Sadira was laying some kind of patch over Landry's wound: one of Mum's regeneration patches, no doubt. Mum and Dad exchanged glances.

Then Dad gave a nod.

"All right," said Mum. "Sadira, you're cleared to go. I'll be along soon."

"I'll help," Sloan offered, stepping forward. But his mother stopped him with a glare.

"You stay put," she commanded. "I don't need help."

She didn't, either. Although she was smaller than Landry, she got him to his feet without any trouble—perhaps because he was becoming more alert. "I'm okay," he said, and "Ouch!" when he touched the patch on his forehead.

"Leave that alone." Sadira braced herself, propping his weight against her shoulder. "Come on."

"I'm fine. Really. I just slipped and hit my head—"

"Right. And there's a procedure for head injuries, like everything else."

"I was feeling sick."

"I know. It's all right. It's an adverse reaction."

Over his feeble protests Landry was led from the room as, one by one, the Bridge crew returned to their checklists. I caught Sloan's eye.

"Happy gas?" I mouthed, jerking my head at the door. Sloan shrugged. Then he cleared his throat.

"Arkwright?" he said loudly. "I need an Array. I can take over the Microorganic reports for you." There was no response. "Arkwright?"

"You do that, Sloan." My dad had heard him, even if Arkwright hadn't. "Use Landry's station. Lais—"

"I'm on it," said Lais. Suddenly everyone was feverishly busy again. Even Mum was back on an Array, frowning at readouts.

I wondered what *I* was supposed to do.

"Uh—Dad?"

No one heard me. Sloan had dashed across to Landry's empty chair. The well-checks were rolling in, each more reassuring than the last. *Okay for power . . . Full integrity for port shields . . . We've got normal status on all processing support systems . . .*

Lais announced that word had come through from Technical Fault Protection. Those energy surges had stopped, she said.

"Dad?" I repeated—and this time he looked around. "Can I do something?"

"Not right now, Cheney." He threw me a distracted smile. "In a minute."

So that was that. I wondered how long it would be until the last status report came through. When that happened, no doubt, the red alert would be over. I settled back into my chair with a sigh.

Once again the expected crisis hadn't occurred. We were still safe and living in a completely stable environment. The thought crossed my mind that nothing *really* bad could ever happen on *Plexus*.

What a fool I was.

Red alert or no red alert, it would be some time before

Arkwright remembered me. That much was clear. My gaze traveled from the back of his head to the back of Sloan's, then across to my mother. I saw fingers fluttering over consoles. I saw glowing digits—layers and layers of them—twinkle and fade and flow through pockets of plasma at various speeds. Voices blended in a complex web of sound as people exchanged comments or murmured into the Audio Interlink Network.

The Public Address System had been shut off.

I was just wondering whether I should give Merrit a call—and Dygall too, perhaps—when my wandering gaze snagged on something peculiar. I sat forward, squinting. Then I got up and went to study the bulkhead more closely.

Over near the toilet cubicle a patch of white wall seemed to be slightly smudged. There was a faint discoloration. At first it looked almost like a scorch mark, with a flush of pale pink at its center instead of pale brown. As I watched, this pink color deepened. Or was I seeing things? I blinked several times—were the edges of the stain expanding? Yes. No.

Yes.

Discoloration was a stress signal. I knew that. The fabric of *Plexus* was designed to display visual changes if its integrity was under threat. Polymer layers responded with optical signals to excessive heat, UV light, chemicals, and other damaging agents. A blue flush acted as a red flag.

But a pink flush? What did that mean?

"Dad?"

Once again no one heard me. After a moment I raised my voice and tried again. *"Dad?"*

"What the hell is that?" said Conal. I was standing near him; he had turned at the sound of my voice. "What have you got there, Cheney?"

"I don't know . . ."

"Tuddor! Look at this!"

The stain was definitely expanding. It was now the size of a basketball. It also had a funny sheen to it—a kind of wet sheen, quite different from the matte finish of the bulkhead.

"Cheney?" said my dad from somewhere behind me. I pointed.

"Look," I said. "What's that?"

No reply. Glancing around, I saw people converging from everywhere: Dad, Mum, Haido . . . even Sloan was heading my way. All eyes were fixed on the pink flush.

"Shit," Dad said, and bumped into the back of someone's chair.

"This can't be good." Conal addressed my mother. "It's a stress signal, isn't it? Color change? It's an integrity warning."

"It can't be," Sloan murmured. He was pressing against my shoulder. "A warning stain would be blue. This isn't blue."

"*Arkwright!*" Dad whirled. "We've got a problem here!"

"Don't touch it!" Mum exclaimed as Sloan bent closer to the bulkhead. "Nobody touch it; stand well away! Cheney—over here! *Now!*"

"What is it?" Dad was talking to Arkwright. He seized my arm, pulling me back into the center of the Bridge. "There's gotta be input, Arkwright; this looks like an integrity breach. So what is it?"

((69))

For the first time ever I saw Arkwright at a complete loss. He peered helplessly across the room, his fine, lank hair in disarray.

"There are no alarms," he insisted.

"There have to be."

"There are *no alarms,* Tuddor. Look for yourself. All the readouts are normal."

Dad released me and strode over to the nearest Interface Array. Meanwhile, Firminus had gotten up and joined his son near the spreading stain.

"Sibber twenty-four linkup." Arkwright spoke into his collar. "Sibber? It's me. Do you have *any* integrity alerts coming in? Any abnormal readings *at all?*"

I didn't hear the reply because Mum was talking from beside the toilet cubicle. "You know," she said, "this looks organic."

"It does," Sloan agreed.

"If CAIP hasn't registered this," said Firminus, "then there's something wrong with CAIP. Arkwright?"

"I heard." Arkwright sounded ever so slightly testy. He addressed Lais. "We'll have to run a full diagnostic," he ordered. "Cyclic redundancy checks, process scans—the lot."

"Roger that," Lais said, and set to work.

"We'll have to isolate the analysis program," Arkwright explained to my father. "I don't know if the problem's in the peripheries, or in the links, or in the CPU itself—I just don't know yet."

"How long will it take to find out?" Dad asked.

"Full diagnostic? About . . . seven, eight minutes?"

"That's a long time, Arkwright."

"We've got another one!" somebody cried. "Report's in from the Health Center! Discoloration on the bulkhead!"

I swallowed. The Health Center? That was on the other side of the ship, practically.

"Sibber's in the same boat," Arkwright announced. "Pink patches in the Depot and pump station three. You'd better talk to him, Tuddor—I'm busy here."

Dad took up the signal link while Arkwright signed off. Sloan had produced a gauge pen, to measure the pink flush. "It's definitely getting bigger," he declared.

"Sloan, will you *stay well back,* please?" My mother was getting irritable. (*The happy gas must be wearing off,* I decided.) "There could be spores. Fumes. Keep well away."

At that point, glancing around the Bridge, I spotted something else. Something very, very unwelcome.

"Uh—Dad?" I quavered. "There's another one."

Chapter Seven

It was right overhead, on the ceiling—a blurred pink ring with a darker center. Everyone looked up. "Oh hell," somebody said. "We're in trouble now."

"None of that!" my father snapped. "Sibber, should we lock down pressure cells?"

"It's contraindicated," Sibber replied through Dad's voice patch. He was Chief Engineer, stationed at the Depot. "We've got more reports coming in from all over the ship—"

"On flash logs?"

"On linkups and Vindow only. If it's an outbreak, we can't contain it anymore; it's moved too fast."

"Are there no system alarms? None at *all*?"

"Not one. Tuddor—we'll have to do manual checks if CAIP's down."

"It's not down," Dad replied. "It's living in a dream world. Lais! What's the status on that diagnostic?"

"Zip." Lais's voice trembled. "Not a twitch. It's reading *total integrity*. Arkwright, this doesn't make *sense!*"

I'd moved away from the pink patch on the ceiling, but I hadn't taken my eyes off it. Like the first, it was growing. Not only that . . .

"It's dripping!" I squeaked. "It dripped!"

"And this one's excreting, too," said Sloan urgently. "Tuddor, I have to get to BioLab. This is organic. This has to be analyzed. Suppose it's a mutant thiocystis bacteria? Suppose it's eating away the fabric of the ship? This looks like organic acid to me."

I saw Firminus glance at his son and frown. But he said nothing. Behind them the glistening pink patch was now almost as big as a man. It was creeping toward the floor. It was . . . bubbling slightly?

"Sloan's right," Mum suddenly declared. "This is a job for Ottilie and BioLab. That radiation's affected the bacteria in the hull."

"Ottilie four oh three linkup!" said Firminus. "Ottilie? It's Firminus. We've got a problem. Ah . . . You, too?"

At that moment my own voice patch beeped. It was Merrit again.

"Cheney?"

"Merrit, this is such a bad time—"

"I know. I realize. But listen—"

"Have you seen it? The stuff on the walls?"

"Yes, I've seen it. It's here. But listen—I just got a funny call from Yestin. He was talking about his Robo-dog—"

"I'm here," Yestin broke in. "I'm linked in. Cheney, there's something wrong with Bam."

"Yestin!" I couldn't believe it. "There's something wrong with the whole *ship!*"

"Yes, that's what I'm saying. I think it's the same thing. He's gone all yellow and soft—"

"He wants to take Bam to BioLab, Cheney," Merrit interrupted. "I don't even know if he's allowed to. Is he?"

"Uh—hang on." I had just realized: Sloan was leaving. He was heading for the door. Dad must have given him clearance. "Sloan! Wait! Where are you going?"

"BioLab," he replied.

"But—"

"It's all right, Cheney." Firminus spoke from behind me. "He won't be going alone."

I looked around in surprise as Firminus brushed past me to join his son. They regarded each other with level gazes. They were exactly the same height.

"It's not necessary," Sloan pointed out.

"Perhaps not to you," Firminus answered in a voice that was quiet but firm.

"Cheney?"

"Merrit, could I just—let me get back to you, okay? There's a lot happening up here."

I wanted to say something to Sloan—I'm not sure what. But he was already stepping through the door ahead of his father. I noticed something odd as the panels met behind them.

Surely those two panels had never come together so *fluidly* before?

((74))

"I think we should seal up again," Mum was saying. "We don't know what this stuff is."

"The atmospheric readouts are fine . . ." Haido remarked.

"Yes, but since CAIP's not functioning properly, that might not mean a thing. Tuddor!"

But Dad was talking to one of his Navvies: the broad-faced girl with the tattooed hairline. "You don't need me," she was insisting, an edge of hysteria in her voice. "This is all data routing stuff."

"We're still at emergency stations—"

"For a cosmic encounter! I do charts! I don't *have* to be here!"

"Look, I'm not going to argue. I don't have time," Dad said shortly. "You do what you think is best."

The tattooed girl seemed close to tears. From his Interface Array Arkwright suddenly remarked, "If she doesn't want to be here, we don't want her here." He wrenched his gaze from the diagnostic readouts. "She won't add value," he explained matter-of-factly.

The tattooed girl gasped; it was as if she had been struck. A call came through from Sibber on Dad's voice patch, and he turned away from her. Mum laid a hand on her shoulder.

"You go," said Mum quietly. "Now."

"I—"

"Go on. Quickly. Go to your husband. I know that's where you want to be."

So the tattooed girl went. And watching her, I was sure of it: something had affected the door. The two panels didn't simply slide apart any longer. They seemed almost to *stretch* apart as if

((75))

they were slightly elastic. As if something were pulling each of them from the middle.

"Dad?" I said, and this time he listened. This time everyone listened. Out of the corner of my eye I saw blurred faces swing toward me.

"Hang on, Sibber. What is it, Cheney?" said Dad. "Have you seen anything else?"

"The door . . ."

"What about the door?"

"It's . . . it's changing."

"It looks yellow," someone piped up.

It did, too. There were yellowish streaks on the white—a kind of blurring around the edges.

"It's not moving right," I pointed out. "It's kind of . . . look." I advanced toward it cautiously. When I crossed the pressure pad, the two panels in front of me practically *peeled* back.

"Bloody hell," said Conal.

"Sibber!" Dad barked. "We have *major structural changes* on the Bridge, here! We're talking *mechanics,* Sibber!"

"Arkwright, we have to seal up!" Mum exclaimed. "At least until we get some results from Ottilie! Arkwright? Are you listening?"

Then Lais shrieked. She jumped from her chair.

Everyone stared—even Arkwright.

"It's sticky!" she wailed.

"What?" said Conal.

"It's sticky! My chair! The armrest! Look!"

I was trying to see what she meant when my voice patch

beeped. I gave a clear-to-send absent-mindedly. I wasn't expecting Dygall.

"Cheney, what's going on?" he demanded. The signal seemed a little rough. A little fuzzy. "Why are the walls changing color?"

"I—we don't know yet—"

"Something's eating up the ship!"

"They're working on it, Dygall."

"I'm fzzchzz . . ."

"What?"

". . . coming over there . . ."

"Dygall—!"

"I'm not sitting around here, waiting for the sczzzz . . ."

"Dygall! Wait! You can't! They won't let you!"

"How are they going to stop me? I'm coming."

"Dygall!"

But he had signed off. And when I tried to call back, he wouldn't give me a clear-to-send.

Dad, meanwhile, was feeling the back of Lais's chair. I heard a slight tearing noise as he pulled his hand away.

"It's tacky," he said in complete astonishment. He looked up, and his gaze met Mum's.

"Look," she said, pointing. "Look at the base." Where the shaft of the chair met the floor, there was a puddle of almost translucent pink material, shot with something hard and yellowish. "It's everywhere."

"Arkwright, get up!" Dad exclaimed. "Everyone get up!"

"The floor as well," Lais whimpered, and she was right.

When I raised my left foot, there was a slight—a very slight—resistance. As if I had honey on the sole of my boot.

Suddenly I was terrified. Truly scared. This was different from the burn. From the emission wave. From anything I'd ever known before.

This was real.

"Mum . . . ?" I croaked, like a little kid, and she came to me. She put her arm around me. I thought, *Get a grip on yourself. Now.*

I took a deep, calming breath.

"I've got a standby alert from BioLab!" Haido said in shaky tones. She, too, was out of her chair, dabbing gingerly at the console. "Ship-wide standby! Stand by for analysis data . . ."

"Ottilie?" Arkwright seemed a bit lost. Without his chair and his console he looked untethered: a thin, gangly figure shuffling around helplessly in front of his Array. "Ottilie, what's the news? Have you got a fix on this stuff?"

The reply, when it came, was on Vindow. Ottilie's head appeared, hovering in plasma: a seamed, drawn, colorless face under a swirl of gray hair. Ottilie was the oldest person on board. She had legs like drinking straws and a voice like the rustle of thermosheets. Behind her I caught a glimpse of BioLab, with all its piping and stowage. The piping looked vaguely odd, I thought. Less defined than usual. Less angular.

"It's protein-based," Ottilie crackled.

"What?" said Arkwright.

"It's protein-based tissue, containing amino acids. Some of the strangest amino acids . . ." She shook her head. "Barely identifiable," she said through tight lips. The picture flickered. "These molecules . . . we're talking transition elements. Metalloids. There's *osmium* in the peptide bonds. *Osmium!*"

I heard Conal catch his breath. "There's osmium in the ship's struts," he gasped. "Tuddor? There's osmium in the casings, I'm sure. Osmium composites."

"Ottilie?" said Dad. "What does that mean, exactly? Are we talking absorption or what? Are we talking metal-eating bacteria?"

The picture broke up for an instant before stabilizing again. Ottilie was frowning. She was shaking her head in perplexity. "We're talking tissue . . . we're talking cells—"

"But what *kind* of cells?" Mum requested. "Bacterial cells?"

"I would say . . . collagenous cells."

"*Collagenous* cells?"

Mum's squawk made us all jump. Ottilie said quickly, "There's no direct correlation, Quenby. This stuff is new; it doesn't fit the traditional classifications . . ." Her picture wavered as Lais turned to Mum.

"What's a collagenous cell?" she asked shrilly.

"Membrane," Mum replied without taking her eyes off Ottilie's distorted form.

"*Membrane?*"

"Ottilie, you're breaking up," said Arkwright. It was true: the picture was deteriorating fast.

Dad said, "Get her on a linkup," and patched through to Sibber. "Sibber?" he said. "Do you have the data through from BioLab?"

"That's affirmative, Tuddor, but—"

"It's protein. Membrane cells."

"Yes, but what do we do? You have to give me something, I can't prep the RARs with this. I need more."

The RARs were our Remote Access Repair Units. They were large robotic troubleshooters, which could be activated in the case of serious impact-based damage or if the nanosystems failed to respond on an atomic level.

Conal shook his head. "Somehow I think it's beyond RARs now," he muttered.

"Hang on—wait." Arkwright was calling for silence. He made a dampening motion with his hand. "Did you say *three* samples, Ottilie?"

". . . fshzzsamples," Ottilie responded from Arkwright's voice patch. Her picture had vanished from the Array, engulfed in random flecks of light. "Two collagenous, one . . . there's a re-semblance to chondrocytes—"

"Cartilage," Mum interjected.

Cartilage? I gaped at her. As in noses? And knees?

". . . some nucleic acids . . ." Ottilie buzzed. ". . . atypical, though, because it's bound up with vshomshh . . ."

"Ottilie? Ottilie!"

"Ark, there's a lot of distortion here," said Lais—and she wasn't talking about the Audio Interlink Network. "Ark, I can't get my *fingers out of the screen!*" But she did—abruptly—yanking them so hard that she stumbled backwards and fell. When she hit the floor, it yielded.

It yielded like sponge.

"Arkwright!" Lais yelped. Her little heart-shaped face was suddenly dead white. She scrambled up, with Conal's assistance. She tried to wipe goo off her hands.

One of Arkwright's staff bolted for the door. I don't know how many people noticed. There wasn't a single challenge as he made his exit. Everyone's attention was fixed on Arkwright.

"Ask her about the fluid!" Mum exclaimed. "Arkwright! Ask her about the excretions: are they toxic?"

"Ottilie! Do you read?"

Through a fuzz of interference came the reply. "Yes, I read you."

Then my own voice patch beeped. Once again it was Merrit. Her signal kept dropping out, like Ottilie's.

"Cheney, it's Merrit—can you hear me?"

"I hear you, Merrit." My lips felt numb.

". . . RARs . . ."

"What?"

"They're malfunctioning!" Suddenly her voice was as clear as a bell. She was sobbing, and my heart almost leaped out of my chest in fright.

"Merrit? *Merrit?*"

". . . Dad saw them! Spraying the struts with acid. Tell Tuddorvzshmmm . . ."

"What? Merrit?"

". . . hydrochloric acid . . ."

The link went dead.

"Merrit? Merrit!" I tapped my collar. "Merrit seven oh five linkup! Hello?"

((81))

But there was nothing.

"Hydrochloric acid?" echoed Mum, who had heard every word. We stared at each other. We both swallowed.

"This diagnostic's stalled, Arkwright!" Lais wailed. "The whole display's a mess. I can't . . . It's all distorted! The plasma's clouding up!"

Arkwright headed straight for one of the junction ports. I knew about them, thanks to his careful training: they were behind an access panel in the bulkhead. When he slapped at the pressure catch, however, the panel didn't behave as expected. Instead of sliding back, it flinched open, like the door. It flinched open like a heart valve I once saw on our mimexic tour of the human body.

The human body?

I looked around as Arkwright plucked a photovoltaic tool from somewhere beneath his pressure suit. The entire compartment was now a different color: no longer white but a strange mixture of slippery pinks, waxy yellows, and livid purples. There were puddles of gloop everywhere. You could vaguely see the dark, stringy shapes of wires and cables through some patches of console, which had lost much of their density, becoming glutinous and transparent. The ribbing of the seams was much less defined. The samplers . . .

The samplers seemed to be throbbing.

"Aagh!"

It was Arkwright. He had opened one of the electrical subconduits, only to be splashed by a spray of fluid. His laser pen clattered to the floor. Gray-faced, he staggered back while the strange, yellowish liquid continued to spurt out of the junction port. It was dripping from his hand; he had apparently removed his glove assembly.

"I—I had to get through the insulation . . ." he croaked.

"Put that under water! *Now!*" Mum cried sharply. She sprang from my side and retrieved Sadira's Medkit. "Is it hurting, Ark-wright? Is it burning?"

"No . . ." He was already stumbling toward the food dispenser. Mum went after him. Dad was staring at the leak, open-mouthed. We all were.

"We—we have to patch it," Conal stammered.

"Quenby! You got a patch there?" Dad exclaimed, and tried once again to contact Sibber. "Sibber twenty-four linkup. *Sibber twenty-four linkup! Hell and damnation—Gower two oh eight linkup!*"

Mum threw a packet of regeneration patches at Conal, who dropped them, picked them up again, and flew toward the junction port. "Keep your gloves on!" Mum cried. I saw other people muttering into their voice patches, trying to make some kind of connection with other parts of the ship. They were edging toward one another, away from the dribbling bulkheads. Some were pulling on their headpieces. Above them . . .

Something moved.

I only just caught it—a flicker that tugged at the corner of my eye. Whipping around, I peered up, fearfully scanning a stretch of slimy ceiling. The seam-ribs bulged palely through a layer of fibrous membrane. Something large and dark and indistinct lurked behind it. (An air duct, perhaps?) There was nothing else

((83))

to see except the samplers. These small round objects—part of the filtration system—had been stuck at carefully calculated intervals all over the various surfaces of *Plexus*. They were designed to analyze the air quality and feed their results back to CAIP via microwaves. They weren't supposed to look like armless jellyfish. Nor were they supposed to be—

"*Moving!*" screamed Lais. "They're *moving!*"

Chapter Eight

The samplers were moving. They were creeping across the ceiling and bulkheads like animated blobs of pink ice cream.

"Yeah," said a voice. "The samplers are crawling around. Didn't you know?"

It was Dygall. I couldn't believe my eyes. And I think Dad, for one, almost had a heart attack.

"Dygall!" he exclaimed, doing an abrupt, one-hundred-and-eighty-degree turn. "Zennor!"

Dygall and Zennor had gotten onto the Bridge—I don't know how. Unless Zennor (who was, after all, a Senate member) had First Level clearance. He stood just behind his son, dragging his fingers nervously through his neatly clipped beard, his dark eyes bloodshot and anxious.

"What—what are you doing here?" Dad demanded.

"I'm sorry, Tuddor, but I couldn't exactly restrain him." Zennor had a beautiful voice, mellow and smooth. Even at that moment, when he was obviously a nervous wreck, I found him soothing to listen to. "It's against the code of ethics—"

"This is *red alert*, Zennor!" Dad boomed. "You have an emergency station and so does he! Where's Darice?"

"Um . . . she's back in Sustainable Services . . ."

"Where *you* should be! Both of you!"

"What's happening in Sustainable Services?" Arkwright wanted to know. Mum was dabbing his left hand dry. "Is it anything like this?" He waved his right hand at the drooling bulkheads, the spongy floor, the discolored ceiling.

"Probably," Dygall replied. "It was better than this when we left, but that was a while ago."

"We got out of our OTV," Zennor explained breathlessly. He was still fiddling with his beard. "We didn't like the look of it."

That made everyone pay attention. "Why?" asked Dad.

Dygall and Zennor exchanged glances. "It was . . . gooey," Dygall said at last.

"It was running off the rails," Zennor added. "I'm sorry, Tuddor. I know we shouldn't be here—"

He yelped then and ducked. We all did. A sampler had whizzed over our heads.

It had flown from one side of the Bridge to the other.

"Oh!" Lais squeaked, and sat down abruptly. She sprang up again at the touch of the sticky, elastic chair with its strange, swollen, pulpy purple cushion. "Oh my God," she whimpered as Haido put an arm around her.

"This is bad," someone murmured. "This is so bad."

There was a brief pause. Finally Haido said in an unsteady voice, "The patch is holding. We've plugged that leak."

"Okay." Dad placed a hand on each temple. "Okay, let's think. Now, Zennor and Dygall got through. That means we can still communicate."

"Reconnaissance parties," said Conal.

"Yes," Dad agreed. "It's vital we keep in contact with Ottilie. Absolutely vital. She's the only one who can give us an answer."

"I'll go!" said Haido.

"Me, too," said the balding Navvy beside her.

"Not me." Arkwright was heading for the junction port again as Mum ordered him to put on his gloves. "I've got to get into CAIP somehow. Without CAIP we're finished."

"All right, you do that." Dad then pointed at the bald man. "Dane, you get to BioLab, see what you can find out, report back here. Like a runner. Understand?"

"Yes."

"*Don't* take the OTVs. Ilaria, you and Feng go to MedLab. Same deal. Zennor—"

"We're not going anywhere," said Dygall flatly. For some reason he crossed the floor to where I was standing. "We're staying right here," he declared, folding his arms. His sweaty scalp gleamed through his ginger fuzz.

"Dygall—"

"Darice will be waiting, son," Zennor remarked. Though his tone was pleasant—reassuring—he was actually wringing his hands. "She'll be waiting for us."

"No, she won't," Dygall retorted. "She'll be trying to fix that busted dispenser."

"Dygall!" Dad barked. He pointed at the door. "Get back to Sustainable Services!"

((87))

"Make me," Dygall growled.

Dad took a deep breath, but before he could speak, Haido stepped forward. "I'll go," she declared.

"And I'll go to TFP," someone else offered, heading for the door. All at once there was movement—a general surge. I couldn't help wondering if some of these people wanted to join their wives and husbands and partners.

Before it was too late.

Dad cried across the milling heads, "TFP's important, okay? TFP might have come up with an alternative comm-link!" That was when I remembered, and touched Dad's arm.

"TFP's in trouble, Dad," I told him. He glanced down at me.

"What?"

"Merrit called. TFP's in trouble." I swallowed. "She said the Remote Access Repair Units were spraying the struts with hydrochloric acid."

"*What?*"

"You mean—like the stuff in our stomachs?" asked Dygall, who had been listening. And Mum, who had also been listening, said, "No. I mean, yes, there *is* hydrochloric acid in our stomachs. But if you're talking about struts, you know what that sounds like?" Her face was suddenly alert, her eyes as bright and sharp as an X-ray scalpel. "That sounds like osteoclasts. That sounds like bone-destroying cells—"

"Wait," said Dad. His scouts were leaving, and he wanted a last word. Chasing them to the door, he barked, "Check the germinators! All the rats and the guinea pigs! Tell Ottilie to monitor them. If there's anything toxic around, they're bound to react!"

Dane raised a hand in acknowledgment before disappearing. Almost at the same instant the door panels uncurled, meeting in front of Dad's face. When the two sides joined, they made a distinct slapping sound. Like wet flesh on wet flesh.

It turned my stomach.

"Now," said Dad, shifting his attention back to my mum, "what was that about bone?"

There were eight of us left on the Bridge: Dad, Mum, Arkwright, Dygall, Zennor, Lais, Conal, and me. We all clustered around Mum, desperate for an explanation—except for Arkwright. Arkwright was absorbed in the junction port.

"Osteoclasts destroy damaged bone with hydrochloric acid," Mum announced. "Then the osteoblasts lay down more collagen and calcium and repair the damage."

"And?" Dad looked lost. His brow furrowed. "How does that relate to anything?"

"I don't know. It's just . . ." Mum waved her hands. "Well, look at all this!" she exclaimed. "It's organic! There's fluid in the cable conduits! There's cartilage in the walls! What does this suggest to you, Tuddor?"

"I—I—"

"This is *organic life!* This isn't bacteria eating the hull; this is something else. This is a *transformation.*"

"But it can't be." Lais gasped. "How can it?"

"Obviously I don't know."

"Wait a minute. Let me get this straight." Even Arkwright was listening. He stood frozen by the junction port, one hand poised over the opening. His great bulging eyes were fixed on

Mum. "Are you saying that we're not dealing with technology anymore?"

"I don't know."

"There are microbes in the hull," Dad observed. "There's DNA in the circuitry. There always was."

"Yes, but did it ever bleed before?" Mum asked.

"What about the lights?" This was Conal. His gravelly voice sounded reassuringly calm. "The lights are still working."

"I don't know about the lights." Mum glanced up, saw a sampler squirming across a light panel, and flinched. "The lights . . . I don't know."

It occurred to me that some bacteria produced light. I had learned about it at school—or was it during my stint in Sustainable Services?

You don't need technology to produce light.

"So, we've got capacitors in CAIP that might have turned into synapses," said Arkwright grimly. "Electrical impulses that might have become chemical ones. Is that what you're saying?"

"I don't know." Mum spread her hands. "It's a possibility."

"Well, that's going to make things difficult," said Arkwright. He turned his head slowly to study the exposed workings of the Bridge. Already to my eyes they looked less like wiring and more like guts. "That's going to make things *very* awkward."

"Look—let's not jump to conclusions," Dad declared. "We can't formulate any sort of deduction without solid, verifiable data. We need Ottilie's input. Ow!" Another sampler skimmed the top of his head, on its way from wall to ceiling. Everyone ducked automatically. We put our hands on our own heads to shield ourselves.

"Then maybe we should *all* go to BioLab," Mum suggested. "If that's where the solution is."

Dad glanced at Arkwright, who sucked in his cheeks. Before Dad could speak, however, someone else did. From behind the door.

"Hello?" said a muffled voice. "*Hello?* Can someone let me in, please?"

I must have squeaked, or jumped, because Mum stared at me. "Yestin!" I exclaimed. "It's Yestin!"

When Conal crossed the pressure pad, nothing much happened. The door panels, which were looking more and more like slabs of muscle, twitched and stretched, but snapped together again instantly.

Then Conal stamped *hard* on the pressure pad, and the panels shrank back once more. Because he stayed where he was, they even remained open. The hole, however, wasn't very big.

Fortunately it was big enough for Yestin. He began to scramble through it.

"Here." Dad darted forward, tripped, then recovered and flung himself against one of the panels. Slowly it yielded to the pressure of his weight, and the hole widened.

I did the same with the other panel. It felt disgusting, even through my glove assembly: taut, slick and rubbery. As I thrust against it, something small and compact leaped past me into the room.

"Bam!" cried Yestin. "Heel!"

"Hell on earth!" Conal exclaimed.

"What's *that*?" yelped Dygall.

"Sorry. He's—I'm sorry." Yestin was now through the hole. His legs looked skinny even though he wore pants *and* a pressure suit; you couldn't, however, see his overdeveloped knees. He had the same bleached, fragile appearance as a bean plant that I once grew for an experiment in low levels of electromagnetic radiation. His hair was almost white. "It's Bam. He's a bit frisky."

"That's your *Robo-dog?*" said Dygall. "But—but—"

"He's changed," said Yestin. It hardly needed pointing out. When I'd last seen Bam, he had been a collection of chips, switches, wires, and panels cobbled together with bits of composite scaffolding and the odd metal pipe. He'd bristled with antennae.

Now he was a ghastly sight, like something half dissected. His pistonettes looked gristly under a thin yellowish membrane. The drum around his microprocessor bore a vague resemblance to some sort of rotten vegetable. His transmission nodes had turned into pulsing red bladders and antennae into—well, one now whipped about like a tail while two others were knitted together by a web of fine, flat, almost translucent fibers, forming something that vaguely resembled an ear.

Yet despite his unfinished appearance, he was skittering across the floor in an excited fashion as people jumped out of his way.

"Bam!" Yestin ordered. "Heel!"

"What—what—" Mum was flabbergasted. We all were. I felt the urge to sit down, but there was nowhere to sit—except on the portable chair.

I realized suddenly that, unlike all the other chairs—which were joined to the floor—the portable chair had not changed. It remained a solid alloy chair.

((92))

And I wondered why.

"He's alive," Yestin explained, pouncing on the rambunctious Robo-dog, which wriggled and barked in his arms. "He's come alive. He's like a real dog."

"He can't be . . ." said Conal hoarsely.

"He is." Yestin spoke in a matter-of-fact tone, gazing up earnestly at the ring of faces surrounding him. "I can tell the difference. You know, originally he was running off photovoltaic cells. Well, I was starting to change that—I wanted him glucose-fueled, like a real dog. Ottilie was helping me. We put a kind of stomach between these two air sockets at the back, and we were working on a miniature glycolysis machine. But we hadn't finished. We hadn't worked out about waste disposal." Yestin was already beginning to look tired; he didn't have the strength to subdue a bundle of energy like Bam. "Well, now he's eating. He ate a biscuit all by himself. And he won't obey me." With a great surge the Robo-dog freed himself. "He always obeyed me before," Yestin added.

Bam spied a moving sampler and began to bark at it. Mum said weakly, "Are you all right, Yestin? You don't look well." Dad was still pushing back his door panel, but his mind wasn't on the job. He wore the expression of someone who'd just been thumped across the head with a blunt instrument.

Dygall announced, "I don't like the look of that door."

I could see what he meant. For a door it was displaying an ominous reluctance to open and shut. I had let go of my panel, and it had snapped back with such speed that I'd barely jumped out of the way in time to avoid being hit.

No one else, however, seemed to be thinking about the door.

"You know," said Arkwright, slowly, "if that robot's become fully organic—"

"Like the ship," Conal interjected.

"—it ought to be taken to BioLab." Arkwright's protuberant gray eyes were fixed on Bam. "That thing might give us the key to this attack. It might be the ship in miniature."

"I *was* taking him to BioLab," Yestin declared, staggering to his feet. "That's where I was going." He looked around. "With Mum and Dad . . ."

"Your parents?" said Dad. He shifted his weight and craned over his shoulder, peering past a muscle flap into the street outside. "Where are they?"

"They were behind me." All at once Yestin sounded anxious. "They were right behind. I had to run after Bam . . ."

He returned to the door, ignoring the sampler that zoomed over his head. Conal joined him, and the three of them—Dad, Conal, and Yestin—struggled with the uncooperative door panels. I glanced at Mum, but her expression wasn't reassuring. She looked shattered, exhausted, and ten years older.

"We ought to get out of here," Dygall suddenly remarked.

"He's right." It was Lais speaking. Her voice was high and nervous. "What if that door stops working? What if we get trapped? We ought to get out while we still can."

"*I'm* going back," said Yestin. He lifted one foot, as if preparing to climb into the street. "I have to find Mum and Dad."

"Wait." Dad grabbed his arm. "Wait, Yestin. Not by yourself."

"I have to!"

"We'll all go. And we'll take the Robo-dog with us." Dad

addressed the whole room; he was red-faced from the strain of holding his side of the door. "I agree with Arkwright," he grunted. "BioLab is where we'll find the answers. It's where we all should be."

"Except that the scouts are going to report back here," Conal pointed out.

"Yes. That is a problem."

"I'll leave my notebook," Zennor offered. He removed from one of his pockets an A4 sheet of plasmafilm, which immediately turned itself on. "I'll write a message and leave it . . . I don't know. On the floor?"

"Is that thing still working?" Arkwright's tone was sharp. Dodging Bam, who was once more scurrying madly around the room, he approached Zennor. "Let me see."

"It's fine," said Zennor, handing over the device. "It hasn't changed."

"That's because it's not attached to the ship."

I was surprised to hear the words come out of my own mouth. The notion had hit me just an instant beforehand; things had come together in my head like chemical reagents, creating a flash. The notebook. The portable chair. There was an absolute logic to it all.

"Anything that's not attached to the ship doesn't change," I observed. "That chair is a discrete object, so it didn't change. Same with the notebook. Arkwright's tools haven't changed. The samplers changed because they're connected through their transmitters. So are the OTVs and the RARs. They're run by CAIP."

When I'd finished, there was a good ten seconds of silence.

Then Yestin said, "But Bam changed. And he's a discrete object. He's got no connection with CAIP at all."

"He's complex, though." Arkwright was thinking hard. I knew the signs: his narrowed eyes, his lowered chin, his quick voice. "That thing's a highly complex mechanism." Arkwright's head jerked up. "It's got to be the *most* complex unattached mechanism on board this ship. In fact, it's the only object that comes *close* to organic potential that isn't already organic—"

"Except for the ship itself," said Mum.

This time the pause seemed to last forever. I found myself lifting my gaze to the ceiling.

Plexus. Our ship. Our *ark.*

An animate being now?

"It was the goddamn life force," Conal said breathlessly. "We hit the goddamn universal life force!" At which point, a sampler whizzed past Dad from the street outside.

Chapter Nine

"Okay," said Dad, "whatever we hit, whatever's happening—"

"We have to get out," Dygall finished.

"Right," said Dad. And we left the Bridge. Slowly, one by one, we clambered through the hole between the door panels. It was becoming so small that by the time Dad squeezed through— nearly falling on his face in the process—the fleshy rims of the panels were sucking at his body.

It was disgusting to watch—like someone being born.

Out in the street there were samplers flying everywhere. The street shuttle had disappeared. All the doors had turned into valves and the floors into slippery paths of tissue, some of it slick and smooth, some of it rough with soggy bristles, some of it bunched into funny pads or pillows that looked a bit like cauliflower heads.

Mum seized my hand.

"I feel as if I'm in somebody's stomach," Dygall muttered,

and I glanced at Mum in alarm. She knew exactly what I was thinking.

"We're not in a stomach," she declared. "If we were, those excretions would be eating through our pressure suits."

"Do you think *Plexus* has a stomach now?"

"I don't know, Cheney."

"What if the streets all fill with fluid?"

"Yeah," said Dygall, lifting one foot. "There's a lot of goo already."

"Let's not worry about that until it happens," Mum replied, and pulled me toward the starboard tube. We all trudged along, glancing nervously from side to side. Yestin cried, "Mum? Dad?" but no one answered. Bam forged ahead, sniffing and scurrying. He made strange clicking noises and occasionally barked.

I was thinking, in a dazed sort of fashion, about *Plexus*. How could something organic survive in space? It wasn't possible, was it? Or was it? If there was osmium in the peptide bonds, perhaps the hull would transform, magically, into an organic shield.

Or would it disintegrate as *Plexus* came fully to life?

I couldn't get my brain around it, somehow. *Any minute, I thought, all this is going to be fixed up. Someone (Arkwright?) is going to work out what to do, and everything will be back to normal.*

I was fooling myself, of course. But perhaps there was no other way of keeping a lid on my own panic.

"What about B Crew?" Lais inquired breathlessly from somewhere behind me.

"There are lots of things we don't know yet," Mum replied in a grim voice. "B Crew's status is one of them."

"Everyone stick together!" Dad exclaimed. "Yestin, did you come from the starboard tube?"

Yestin nodded.

Walking was difficult on the uneven surface of the floor, but we finally reached the starboard tube. Standing at the junction, we looked to our left and our right but saw no one else. There was nobody on the platform, nobody down in the tube itself—which was now lined with ribbed, resiny material. The great arching space was empty as far as the curve of the ship's drum allowed us to see.

Yestin said, "Where are Mum and Dad?"

"They might have turned down one of the streets," Zennor suggested.

"Why?"

"Well—I don't know, but—"

"They were right behind me. They were heading for BioLab."

"Did you tell them you were going to stop at the Bridge?" Mum queried. "You were chasing your Robo-dog, weren't you? Perhaps they didn't see you turn. Perhaps they had to check down each of the streets between here and BioLab."

"Can we look for them?" Yestin asked, and Dad put a hand on his shoulder.

"We have to get to BioLab, Yestin," he said. "If your parents aren't there already and we don't pass them on the way, we'll send someone back to look."

"They'll be all right," Mum added.

The words were barely out of her mouth when we heard a scream. It was very faint, but it was definitely a scream.

And it was the most frightening thing I'd ever heard in my life.

"Oh my God," Lais breathed.

"Mum? Dad?" shrieked Yestin, and grabbed my dad's arm. "Who was that? Was that them?"

"I—I don't know . . ." Dad stammered. Then Conal started to run toward the noise, which had come from the direction of GeoLab, off to our left. "Conal?" Dad cried. "What are you doing?"

Conal paused. He half turned.

"We should stick together," said Mum in an unsteady voice.

"Wait." Dad suddenly took charge. "You're right—we should stick together. Plus Arkwright and Quenby have to get to Bio-Lab. The kids, too. Lucky it's in the right direction—"

"But what about my mum?" Yestin wailed.

"I'll take care of your mum," said Conal. Though small, with sloping shoulders and short legs, he suddenly looked heroic. "Give me that laser pen, Arkwright," he added. "Just in case. I'm sure I won't need it—"

"I'll go with you," Dad interjected. Before Mum could protest— I heard her catch her breath—Conal said, "No."

"But—"

"I don't have a kid, Tuddor," Conal pointed out quietly. Whereupon Arkwright handed over his laser pen.

Dygall croaked, "We need some guns," but I don't think anyone heard him. Except me. And perhaps his father.

Zennor frowned.

Dad said, "Give it ten minutes, Conal. *Ten minutes.* Then come back to BioLab."

"Right."

"And if you see anyone else, pass the word. BioLab."

Conal nodded. He headed off down the tube as samplers banked and soared around him.

"Try not to touch anything!" Mum called, and Conal lifted a hand.

"That scream was probably just someone getting a shock," Lais quavered. "Like I did when my chair went sticky."

"Yes, I'm sure that's right." Zennor spoke in a soothing manner, putting his arm around Yestin. "Everyone's in a highly agitated state. You have to remember that."

Yestin gazed up at him, with a look of hope dawning on his face. Dygall rolled his eyes. Dad prodded my arm. "Come on, everyone," he said. "We can't afford to hang around."

So we pressed on toward BioLab, with many a backwards glance. Finally we lost sight of Conal. Dad was in the lead, followed closely by Lais. Mum and I were next in line. Zennor followed us, between Dygall and Yestin. Arkwright brought up the rear. He seemed to be thinking.

At the next junction Dad checked the street to our right, but it was empty. He even yelled hello and waited for a moment in case there might be a reply. There wasn't. He did the same whenever we reached a junction, with no success. We were passing through pressure cells designed for storage: chemical components, spare parts, gas cylinders—nothing that was going to yell back.

The residential areas that we passed were empty, too. Their inhabitants were probably at emergency stations somewhere else on board. We didn't see a single street shuttle or On-board Transport Vehicle. Just lots and lots of samplers.

Bam kept chasing the samplers, so that Dygall had to call him to heel repeatedly. Yestin didn't. For the first time Yestin seemed to have forgotten his Robo-dog. He staggered along looking stunned.

"That Robo-dog might tell us a lot," Arkwright murmured, and raised his voice. "We should have a good look at it, Quenby, when we reach BioLab!"

"Sure."

"If the CPU's turned into a neurological network, I'm going to need all the help I can get," Arkwright went on.

I noticed that he kept lagging behind, lost in mental calculations. "We'll have to work together. I'm not very clear on things like the central nervous system or even the autonomic nervous system—is that what it's called?"

"Yes," said Mum. "But *Plexus* isn't normal. We can't assume anything."

"No. I know."

"I really don't see—I mean, it's going to be so hard—"

"Ow!"

Ahead of us Lais had run into Dad, who had stopped short. Bam was barking frantically. We all looked up.

A large shape was scuttling across the ceiling. I knew instantly what it was. Though it had slipped off its circuit rail, and its boxy composite sheath was now a kind of elastic shell, and its suction-valve brushes had turned into beating hairs, or cilia, and its padded wheels had transformed themselves into sucker-like attachments, I still recognized the grayish sheen and distinctive shape of a Remote Access Laundry Unit.

It seemed to pause overhead, its cilia pulsing.

Everyone froze. It was an instinctive reaction. To see something so big—so big and *alive*—touched the primitive *Homo sapiens* in all of us.

Dad was the first to come to his senses.

"Okay," he muttered without taking his eyes off the RAL. "Okay, everyone, let's keep going. Gently, now. Gently . . ."

Before we could move, however, the RAL's suction valve convulsed. It disgorged a great blast of glossy blue discs, each about the size of my palm. They poured out but didn't pick up much speed. They just floated in the air, rippling slightly. Slowly they began to disperse.

They looked vaguely familiar.

"Wh-what?" Lais stuttered.

"Just move!" Dad snapped. "BioLab! *Move!*"

"Scent pellets." I gasped. "Could they be scent pellets?"

"*Move,* Cheney!"

They *were* scent pellets—I was sure of it. I had studied the laundry system during my stint in Sustainable Services. All RALs carried scent pellets. When you didn't clean with water, scent pellets were vital.

But I didn't get the chance to have a really good look. We were already moving, running along the tube toward BioLab. I stumbled and nearly fell. Mum hauled me to my feet again.

"Mum—"

"Later!"

We charged down the platform, though there was no need to. The RAL didn't follow us; I glanced back to check. It was disappearing down one of the streets, leaving a trail of drifting scent pellets.

Ahead of me Dad slipped. It was easy to do on that surface. He hit one knee coming down and swore. Lais careened into him; she also tumbled.

"It's all right!" Zennor said panting. "It's gone!"

"Slow down." Mum was also gasping for breath as she hung off my arm. "We can't—can't run—we'll hurt ourselves—too uneven . . ."

"I want my mum . . ." Yestin whimpered.

"What *was* that thing?" Dygall exclaimed wildly. "What was it doing?"

"It was a Remote Access Laundry Unit." I was surprised that he hadn't worked it out. "And those blue things were scent pellets. At least they *used* to be . . ." I saw one flit by, dodging a sampler, and added desperately, "I—I don't know what they are now."

"Enzymes, perhaps?" Arkwright speculated, his blank gaze fixed on the same pellet. "Hormones?"

"It doesn't matter," Lais said. "Come *on.*"

"Of course it matters." Arkwright spoke quite sharply, for him. "Everything matters. We can't deal with any of this unless we know what's going on."

"Well, whatever those blue things are, they don't look dangerous," Zennor remarked, sounding more hopeful than relieved. "There's no reason to think they're dangerous."

"Perhaps we ought to catch one," Arkwright suggested. I knew what he meant, I knew he was right, but I couldn't dredge up much enthusiasm. Harmless or not, the scent pellets were strange and disquieting.

I just wanted to get away from them.

Fortunately Dad said, "Not now. Later. We haven't even got a sample box with us."

"When we reach BioLab," Mum added, "we can work out exactly what we need."

So we pressed on, cautiously. I found myself watching the area above my head. Dad began to approach every junction with more care, even though—as Zennor had pointed out—there was no reason to regard the scent pellets (or the samplers, for that matter) as dangerous. They all seemed to be going about their mysterious business as if we weren't there.

"It's like being Jonah inside the whale," Lais muttered at one point.

"Huh?" said Dygall.

"Jonah. You know. From the Bible."

Dygall didn't know. Neither did I. Though we had done a unit on the Bible in our history course, neither of us could remember any Jonah.

"He was swallowed by a whale," said Lais. "He lived inside it for a while."

"And then what happened?" I asked.

Lais hesitated. "Actually," she admitted, "I don't really know . . ."

"He was vomited up onto dry land." It was Zennor who spoke. "The Lord made him preach outside Nineveh."

"Well," said Dygall, "I hope that doesn't happen to *us*. Unless we find the right sort of dry land."

"It's a story about trying to avoid your destiny," Zennor began—and was suddenly hit.

A scent pellet hit him. It exploded against his back in a cloud of fine blue powder. He dropped to his knees from the impact.

Lais screamed. *"Zennor!"* she cried.

The smell was very strong. It was vaguely soapy and a little bit herbal, with a touch of citrus thrown in. Zennor climbed to his feet again. "It's all right," he said, gasping. "I'm fine . . ."

"Did it get on your skin?" Mum demanded. "Zennor?"

"I—I don't know—"

"There's a bit on his neck," Arkwright pointed out. "And in his hair."

"Wipe it off! Quick!" said Mum.

"It's okay. It didn't really hurt. It—it just pushed me over."

"Don't anybody breathe it in!" Mum cried.

We all stepped back, though the powder had pretty much settled. Most of it was on Zennor's pressure suit: the mark looked like a big blue flower. Mum tried to dust it off, using her glove assembly. But it was faintly moist and stuck like glue.

So did the smell.

"You should take that suit off," Mum suggested.

Dad, however, said, "Not now. We're nearly there."

"It might be toxic—"

"He's not dead yet," said Dad. "Come on. He'll need to wash it out of his hair, anyway."

"It must have been a clumsy pellet," Dygall interjected shrilly. He was worried about his father; I could tell from the way he was standing. But he didn't want to show it. "Dad must have gotten in its way, and it smashed."

"I'm fine," Zennor repeated.

Dad was already forging ahead, and Lais had started to move, too. Arkwright hovered at Zennor's elbow.

"Can you walk?" he inquired.

"Yes, of course," Zennor replied, and began to shuffle forward. Mum told Arkwright to go on—*she* would stay with Zennor. She didn't want anyone else getting too close to him.

I touched Dygall's arm. "Come on," I said. "We mustn't lose my dad."

Up at the front of the line Dad had reached the next junction. He stopped. Cautiously he peered around the street corner, crying, *"Hello!"*

Then he jerked back so abruptly that he trod on Lais's foot.

"Ow!" she yelped.

He didn't say sorry. I don't think he could. He had swung around to face her, gasping, wide-eyed. As we watched, he collapsed against a wall.

But when Lais tried to pass him, his arm shot out.

"No!" he choked.

"What—"

"Don't. Wait. Please . . ."

Now we all knew that something was wrong. We slowed. We halted. We stared.

"What is it?" Lais whispered.

Dad swallowed. He seemed to have aged ten years in ten seconds.

"An—an accident . . ." he said hoarsely.

"What?"

"Don't look down the street." He straightened and addressed us all. "We—we have to cross this junction, and BioLab's just four more streets away. You kids—when we cross this junction, I want you to shut your eyes . . ."

"Why?" Arkwright queried. Mum gave him a vicious jab before jerking her head at Yestin. Yestin gasped.

"It's Mum!" he squeaked.

"No," said Dad. "Yestin—"

"It is!" Yestin cried, then surged forward. It happened so quickly that Dad wasn't fast enough to stop him. Yestin flung himself around the corner, just behind his Robo-dog. What he saw made him stop—but it didn't stop Bam.

By the time I hit that junction, pulling against my mother's grasp, Bam had reached the corpse that lay halfway down twenty-first street.

He began to bark excitedly.

Chapter Ten

I'll never forget that moment. It changed everything. I saw the
body, and everything else seemed to fade into the background. I
knew that things would never be all right ever again. I knew
that the old world was gone.

And I was right.

The body didn't belong to either of Yestin's parents. I saw that
instantly, because the face was still intact. It was Haido, and
she was dead. Most of her middle part was gone—burned or
melted away.

You could smell it. That smell. It makes me sick even now.
Just to think of it.

Yestin threw up. Right then, in front of me. I shut my eyes,
but of course it was too late. That carnage is seared into my
mind, and I can't get rid of it.

I wish I hadn't looked. I wish I'd done what I was told.

"No—no—"

I don't know who was whimpering. It could have been anyone. Dad—I'll never forget this—Dad moved past me, and said, "It's not your mother. Yestin? It's not your mother. Look at me, son."

"Cheney? Come on." Mum was able to talk. Her voice was hoarse, but she was Chief Medic. She had seen dead bodies before. She could cope with them. "Over here. *Now.*" She took my hand. She began to lead me away.

Lais was crying. I could hear her. Dygall . . . I opened my eyes and found myself looking at Dygall. He was standing as if frozen, staring, white-faced with Zennor's arms twined around him from behind.

"Come," Zennor croaked. "We can't do anything for her."

"We have to get out of here!" Lais sobbed. "Tuddor! These streets aren't safe!"

"Wait." Only Arkwright sounded calm. "We have to bring Haido."

"*What?*"

"We have to, Lais. We have to find out what did this."

"It's true," Mum agreed. We had already left the junction, she and I, but she turned back. She retraced her steps, dragging me with her. "That's true. We need to know. Tuddor—"

"I'll do it." Dad gave Yestin a gentle push. "Go on. You go with Quenby."

"Mum . . ." Yestin sobbed. "Where's my mum?"

"Go on, Yestin," Dad urged. "She's probably in BioLab."

"Come on, sweetie," said Mum. "That's a good boy . . ."

When Yestin reached us, I put an arm around his shoulder.

I said, "You stay with me. We'll be all right." My voice wobbled a bit—I felt as if I could hardly breathe—but I did it. I talked.

So did Dygall.

"We need guns!" he wailed.

"Okay, go," said Dad. He picked up Haido's feet. He was going to drag her along the floor.

I looked away.

"Was it acid?" Arkwright asked Dad.

"We'll find *out*, Arkwright. Just *go!*"

Lais had already gone. She was way ahead of us by that time. I kept a firm grip on Yestin, whose body shuddered with every wrenching sob. I wasn't crying, myself. I don't know why. Too shocked, perhaps.

"You kids," Mum said, panting, as we hurried along, "you kids, if you see any . . . remote units . . . you duck into the nearest cabin. Or a stair shaft . . . compartment . . . anything. Get in there and shut the door . . ."

"Did—did a rem—remote do that?" Yestin hiccupped.

"I don't know," said Mum.

"It could have been a sampler that did it!" Dygall exclaimed. "It could have been anything!"

"Wait." Lais stopped abruptly. We all did because she was in front and had reached the next junction.

Dad was bringing up the rear. When I glanced over my shoulder, I saw him. He was shuffling backwards, dragging his burden. Blocking it from view.

"Well?" said Mum. "Lais?"

"Nothing," Lais croaked. She had edged around the corner. "It's—it's clear."

"Go, then!"

Lais went. Mum and I followed, with Yestin. Zennor and Dygall were right on our heels.

Then Bam shot past, dashing ahead, barking merrily. He shot down the platform (making pads of flesh wobble under his strange, chicken-leg feet), halted, turned, and shot back again. He kept doing it, as if he was impatient. Lais said wildly, "I wish that damn thing would *shut up* . . ."

"It's not a damn thing, it's a good thing." Mum coughed.

"It's making too much noise!"

"It'll draw fire," said Dygall faintly. "Can't you see? It'll get hit first because it'll attract the most attention."

"Oh." Lais subsided.

"Anyway," said Mum, "we don't know how . . . I mean, it might not be the noise that . . ." She, too, subsided, but I knew what she meant. Bam was our early warning system.

We had reached the next junction.

"It's clear," announced Arkwright, who had overtaken the rest of us. Just looking at him, I felt safer. There was something about Arkwright. In the midst of this chaos his mind was still working calmly. He had always been that way; his intellect was so active, his curiosity so rampant, that he didn't seem affected by the concerns of ordinary people. He was too interested to be afraid.

"Tuddor? How are you doing?" he asked, stretching up to peer over the top of my head.

"Fine," came Dad's muffled response.

"Need help?"

"No."

Then Lais shrieked. When I swung around, the air was full of blue powder. Someone had been hit—another scent pellet.

Arkwright? No. Lais.

"Oh no! Oh no!" she cried, coughing and waving her arms. Her face, hair, and back were streaked with blue. "Quenby! Help! Quenby!"

"It's all right." Mum let go of my hand. "Don't panic—"

"Help me! Help!"

"Don't *panic!*" Dygall snapped. "Didn't you *hear?* It doesn't *hurt* you! Dad's *fine!*"

Lais was groaning and shaking. Mum was trying to dust her off. Zennor said, "Come *on*. We can't stop!"

From down in the rear Dad lifted his voice. "Keep moving! Everyone keep moving; we're nearly there!"

Arkwright was the first to move. He marched across the next junction while Bam capered around his ankles. I held on tightly to Yestin and followed. Mum was just behind me, holding Lais. Then came Zennor and Dygall. Dad struggled along in last place, panting and grunting.

Samplers and scent pellets swirled overhead. I tried to keep an eye on them, but it was impossible. There were too many, and the samplers were too fast. Some of them were even sliding along the bottom of the tube.

I kept saying to myself, *We're going to make it. We're going to make it.* Over and over and over again.

"Hang on, Tuddor." It was Zennor speaking. "You'll never keep up."

Peering behind me, I saw Zennor drop back to help with Haido. He tucked his hands under her arms and lifted her until she was fully off the ground. Mum said, "Don't touch anything! Mind that stuff . . . watch her middle . . ."

"It's all right." Dad gasped. "We're nowhere near the wound."

"Two more streets," Arkwright remarked. "Only two more."

I thought, *And then what?* It was the first time I'd even stopped to wonder. Suppose we reached BioLab and it was empty? Suppose everyone was dead in there as well? Acid. Someone had mentioned acid. Hydrochloric acid? Had the Remote Access Repair Units stopped spraying struts and started spraying people?

I felt a lump rising in my throat before it hit me: Sloan was in BioLab. Sloan was waiting for us. I was able to swallow the lump when I remembered that, because Sloan couldn't be dead. Not Sloan. *He* would take care of things; nothing ever fazed him. Together he and Dad and Arkwright would work out a solution.

And Mum, too, I decided. They would save us. They would.

We passed another junction. Everyone was breathing heavily. Lais had calmed down a bit. Arkwright was lengthening his lead, walking briskly, apparently lost in thought. (I couldn't *believe* how cool he was.) Yestin sniffed, wiping his nose on his hand. Once he whimpered, "My mum," and I gave him a squeeze.

"She'll be all right," I said automatically, without believing a word of it.

No one else said anything. What was there to say? We were dragging a corpse with us—we didn't want to look back. We could barely open our mouths. Perhaps we were all in shock; I don't know. Perhaps we were a little sick. *I* certainly was. The smell was getting to me: the sickly, dreadful, burned-meat and chemical smell that kept wafting past me from Haido's direction.

My mouth was dry. My heart was hammering. The blood was pounding in my head.

As we crossed the next junction, I felt dizzy for a moment. I actually stumbled on something that looked almost like one of the limestone rock formations I'd seen in a mimexic caving tour. I think it was called a shawl. On the tour it had been hard: a very thin and brittle sheet of calcite, almost like a petrified curtain.

The one I tripped over was soft and springy. Like the webbing you have between your toes.

"Cheney! Are you all right?" said Mum.

"I'm fine."

"Cheney?"

"I'm fine, Dad! It's okay!"

"Just a few more steps, kids! Not long now!"

It was true. We were close, so close. Arkwright was actually *turning onto twenty-sixth street.* I think we picked up our speed. I'm pretty sure I did.

But it was too late.

We weren't fast enough.

I never saw it happen. When I heard the screams and whipped around, it was already over. Zennor was on the ground. Rolling and writhing—bucking. The noise was—I can't even describe it. I can't. He had been hit in the face, full on. He was *bubbling*. *Steaming*.

I barely caught a glimpse. Then I was being hauled backwards. Someone grabbed me: Arkwright. He seized my arm and Yestin's, and he pulled us along. We ran. We had to. When Yestin fell, Arkwright jerked him up again with the kind of strength that I *never* would have expected. Yestin was screaming. I might have been screaming—I don't know. I couldn't understand what was going on.

I saw a familiar face: it belonged to Firminus. He was there suddenly. Arkwright practically threw me at him; I flew straight into his arms with a thump, nearly knocking him over. He caught me and shoved me at a hole in the wall. A *door* in the wall. The BioLab door.

Sloan was on the other side of this hole. He was propping it open.

"Zennor!" I cried.

"Quick," said Sloan. He reached across. He grabbed a handful of my suit and yanked me through the hole. I hit the floor inside on my hands and knees. Yestin was so close behind, he nearly fell on top of me.

"Sloan . . ." I sobbed.

"It's all right." Sloan's voice was perfectly calm. "It's all right; you're both safe."

"Mum!" I gasped. "Dad!"

"They're coming."

"He's dead!"

"Shh."

Looking around, I saw faces. Scared expressions. I recognized Ottilie; her hair was coming down. I didn't really know the other three. I may have seen them in the tubes or at the Health Center, but I didn't know who they were.

All at once a roiling mass of limbs seemed to burst through the hole behind me. It was Firminus holding Dygall. Dygall was shouting and struggling. He was kicking and screaming. *"Dad!"* he shrieked. *"Dad!"* His elbow hit Firminus on the cheek, but Firminus didn't let go. Knocked backwards into a slimy bulkhead, he slid to the floor, still holding on tight, his arms locked around Dygall's chest. "Shh," he said desperately. "Shh."

"Dad! Da-a-a-ad!"

Yestin was shocked into silence. I crawled across to Dygall. I didn't know what to do, but I had to be there. I didn't even think—I just moved.

"Dygall . . ." I croaked.

He kicked out at me. I doubt he even realized who I was. It was so noisy, he probably hadn't even heard me speak. Firminus pressed his cheek against Dygall's fuzzy scalp and held on grimly. Yestin began to howl.

"They're not here!" he cried. "Mum and Dad! They're not here! Oh no! Oh *no!*"

"Shh. Shh." I didn't even know what I was saying. An almighty thump made me turn around. It was Zennor. Arkwright and Tuddor had lost their grip, and he'd hit the floor. They had rushed him into BioLab.

"Oh my God . . ." someone breathed. Everybody was inside

now; only Haido had been left in the street. The door had snapped shut. Lais was in hysterics, screaming at the top of her lungs. Mum was crouching over Zennor, blocking my view. (I'm so grateful that she blocked my view.) She was slicing through his suit with something—something Ottilie had given her. The smell was appalling. Zennor's hand was twitching.

"DA-AD!" Dygall screeched. With one huge convulsive movement he jerked out of Firminus's grasp. He launched himself at his father. I was in his way, though, and I grabbed him. I grabbed his collar.

His fist shot out. It hit my nose.

I saw flashes of light.

"Cheney!" Dad's voice cut through all the commotion. He was there suddenly; I felt his bulk at my side. He lifted me up. We moved. He sat me down somewhere.

"Are you all right? Cheney?"

"Ow . . . ow . . ."

"Show me. Let me look."

I uncovered my nose. He turned my head this way and that as my vision cleared. Close up, his face was a shock. He looked wild. There were angry red spots on his jaw. His eyes stared. I realized that I was moaning.

"It's not broken." He wheezed. "Quenby? It's not broken. It's not even bleeding."

"Dygall . . ." I tried to look around Dad, but he wouldn't let me.

I heard someone say, "Get those kids out of here."

"Yes." That was Ottilie. "In there. Take them into the Pen."

The Pen was where Sustainable Services kept all the germinators: the rats, the guinea pigs, the plankton, the racks and racks of molds and lichen and algae and mosses. The germinator tanks were built into the walls on all sides. It was one of my favorite rooms on board *Plexus,* because it was full of birdseed and hamster wheels and other fun things. Beyond it—through a small door with a First Level clearance lock—lay the Gene Banks. The Gene Banks contained DNA samples from every species on Earth.

There was also a small collection of large living animals (apes, sheep, and so forth), but they weren't kept in BioLab. They were in the Stasis Banks, with B Crew. Animals could be kept in cytopic suspension indefinitely, because it didn't matter what happened to their brains. They were needed only for breeding purposes.

"What was it?" I quavered, allowing myself to be led from the laboratory into the Pen. A sampler flashed past, and I winced. "Dad? What happened to Zennor?"

"Shh."

"Tell me! What *did* that? Tell me, Dad!"

"It was a sampler."

"A *sampler?*"

"It's all right—"

"There are samplers in *here!*"

"We'll catch them. We'll get rid of them."

"We haven't had any problems with the samplers," said Ottilie, sounding dazed. "Not a thing . . ."

"It's all right. Cheney, it's all right." We hugged each other,

Dad and I, rocking back and forth. I couldn't seem to let him go. We were sitting on the floor of the Pen surrounded by tanks. The glass in these tanks was no longer transparent; it had turned into a cloudy sort of membrane. I could hear someone wailing— it was Dygall—and I tried to bury my head in my father's chest. But I couldn't block out that terrible sound.

"Shh," he said. "Shh."

"Oh no . . . oh no . . ."

"We're okay. We're okay now."

"Zennor."

"I know."

"Dygall . . ."

"I know."

"What happened?" It was Sloan's voice. Sloan was nearby.

I pulled away from my father. Something about the sound of that gentle question made me feel that I shouldn't be cringing on the floor. I didn't want Sloan to see me in such a state.

Looking up, I saw that he was standing over us.

"What happened?" he repeated. "Zennor was attacked?"

"It was a sampler," Dad replied.

"A *sampler?*"

"Out of the blue." There was no strength in Dad's tone. He pressed the heels of his palms into his eyes. "It just—sprayed him. This little thing. *Liters* of the stuff."

"What stuff, Tuddor?"

"I—I don't know . . ." Dad looked toward the door of the Pen. Ottilie was bringing Yestin through it. She sat him on a stool—a stool that was still a stool rather than a fleshy nub—and gave him a cup of water. A cup of water and a pill. "You take this," she murmured. "Go on. Take it."

But Yestin couldn't take it. He was shaking too much to hold a pill. Ottilie had to pop it into his mouth and press the cup to his lips. He nearly choked on its contents.

"Water?" Dad croaked.

"We've tested it," Ottilie replied.

"You mean your *instruments* are working?"

Ottilie looked up. Wisps of gray hair framed her face. "No," she said quietly. "Most of them aren't. We had to use germinators."

Suddenly the air was split by an unearthly cry. It was so awful, I had to put my hands over my ears. Ottilie shut her eyes, and Yestin whimpered. Even Sloan bit his lip.

Dygall had been told that his father was dead.

Chapter Eleven

Mum didn't give Dygall a sedative pill. She gave him a sedative *gel,* which she dabbed under his nose. Within seconds he was quiet—almost groggy—despite the fact that he'd wiped off most of the gel as soon as Mum's back was turned.

Her back was turned because she was trying to work out what should be done with Zennor's body. I could hear her discussing it in the other room. None of the Shifters was allowed in the other room while Zennor was there. Mum didn't even want any *adults* going near the remains. (That was what she called his body.) She wanted to isolate Zennor, just in case.

"This stuff on his face might be unstable. The fumes might be dangerous," she said.

"We could analyze it," Ottilie responded. "We can't use the spectrometer, and the ion-channel biosensors are out, but we've got one or two portables, and all our solutions are intact . . ."

"Fine," said Mum. "You can take a sample, but I still want him isolated. *Now.*"

"But where?" I didn't recognize the voice. It was a man's voice. "The germinator tanks aren't big enough."

"Outside? In the street?" someone else suggested.

"Not an option." It was Firminus speaking. He sounded very tired. "We can't get through the door anymore."

"What?" said Mum.

"The door's in lockdown mode. We just disabled the pressure pad."

"Why—how—?"

"I stuck a magnetron pole through it."

"We can't afford to let any more samplers in," Arkwright declared. Everyone accepted that. There was a brief pause.

"Could we put Zennor in another pressure suit?" Ottilie finally suggested. "And seal it up?"

"You saw what happened to the last pressure suit," Mum replied. "Anyway, it would require too much handling. I don't want anyone touching that stuff."

"Air duct?" said someone.

"Contaminate an air duct? Are you kidding?"

"Precision pipe." It was Sloan's voice. Looking around, I saw that he wasn't anywhere near me and realized that he must have slipped back into the lab. "What about the precision pipe?" he suggested. "That was built to hold a vacuum—it belongs to the particle accelerator module—"

"Good idea," Ottilie cut in. "We'll put him in there. Jehanne? Castus? You do it."

"No," said Dad. "*I'll* do it." He had been very quiet. Like Firminus, he sounded exhausted. "You people have your own jobs to do. We need to know what we're dealing with. We need more analysis."

"We need CAIP," Arkwright stated flatly.

"Right. So you'd better access it somehow."

"I'll need help for that," said Arkwright. "If I'm dealing with a central nervous system instead of a CPU—"

"*I* can help you," Mum interjected. "I've been thinking: when a nerve wants to pass a signal to another nerve, it releases acetylcholine—a neurotransmitter. If we can start with that and—I don't know—work out a kind of chemical signal code, to get your message through—"

"Without a projection program?" someone said. "Without any kind of molecular models? How are we going to design it?"

"As best we can," Mum snapped.

"All right," said Dad wearily. "I'll take care of Zennor. You and Arkwright start on CAIP. You may need Ottilie's input—"

"No problem." Ottilie had a soft, precise little voice, but it seemed curiously strong and firm compared to a lot of the others. Even Firminus was beginning to sound shaky. "We already have some data," she said. "Jehanne's our tissue expert. Sloan—you can take care of that toxin analysis."

"Right."

"What about the Robo-dog?" Arkwright was speaking. "He might be the best chance we have. What if he's the ship in miniature?"

There was a brief silence. I glanced at Yestin, who was sitting right next to me. We were still in the Pen, of course; no one would let us out. Lais was with us, huddled beside Yestin. She had her arm around his shoulders. We were all three slumped against a bench unit that, because it was on wheels, had not been transformed. It remained an ordinary bench, complete with drawers full of pipettes and petri dishes.

I knew that occasionally Ottilie had performed dissections on top of this bench. And I also knew that Yestin would never allow Bam to be dissected.

The Robo-dog was now sprawled near Yestin's feet. Its glistening flanks rose and fell as it breathed. The very fact that it was sitting there finally convinced me: Bam was alive. No robot dog should ever need to rest. Yet there was Bam, resting.

His master was also resting. Poor Yestin looked really sick. His color—or lack of it—was awful. He kept sighing and sniffing. He stared dully across the room.

Beside him Lais didn't look any better. She, too, had been given a sedative.

"Excuse me." Sloan was squeezing past our feet. Glancing up, I saw that he was carrying a piece of equipment. "Could I put this down here? Thanks."

"What is it?" I inquired as he placed the instrument on top of the bench.

"Portable biosensor."

"What are you going to do with it?"

"Check a sample." Sloan glanced over at Dygall, who had dozed off in one corner. Then he turned back to me and lowered his voice. "Toxin sample," he added. "From Zennor's face."

"Oh."

I got up then. I was feeling a bit calmer, despite the samplers that were crawling around overhead. Every few seconds I would glance at the ceiling, just to keep track of where they were.

Sloan followed my gaze.

"They haven't been giving *us* any trouble," he assured me.

"Doesn't mean they won't."

"Possibly." Sloan transferred his toxin sample, inserted the slide into its slot, and powered up. "I'd certainly like to know what's going on with those samplers," he mused. "They're just overblown biosensors—or they *used* to be. Protein-based ion channels inside lipid membranes, with a metalloy/bacteriorhodopsin composite coating. So how come they've started squirting people with organic acid?"

"Maybe we ought to catch one," I murmured, my eyes still fixed on the ceiling.

"Maybe. I wouldn't like to try, though. Suppose they start defending themselves?"

"We need guns," someone mumbled.

It was Dygall, of course. He was awake again. Sloan and I both looked over at where he was curled up near a plankton tank.

He gazed back at us blearily.

"We need guns," he repeated with some effort. "Weapons . . ."

"Take it easy, Dygall," said Sloan.

"*Charge* guns!"

"We can't go letting off bursts of electromagnetic radiation," Sloan pointed out. His tone was distracted, because his attention was once more focused on the work in front of him. "It wouldn't be safe."

"Safe?" squawked Dygall, and coughed. "*Safe?* What are you *talking* about, you idiot? This whole ship's probably going to collapse any minute!"

"Not necessarily."

"We're in *space!* Living things can't *survive* in space!"

"This one was designed to." Sloan adjusted something on his biosensor, speaking gently. "Anyway, there are some pretty tough organisms around, remember. We've used them ourselves."

"What's the *matter* with you?" Dygall protested. "Are you crazy? Can't you see what's happened? People are dying!"

"Hey." I went over to Dygall. He was my Little Brother, after all. "Do you want a bite to eat?" I asked, crouching next to him. "We can still use the food dispenser. Peanuts and things— Ottilie's tested them out on the germinators."

"Cheney . . ." His eyes filled with tears. "My dad's dead," he whispered.

"I know." What could I do? I squeezed his arm. "I'm so sorry, Dygall."

"We're all dead."

"No."

"We're all going to die," he insisted, and laughed. It was a terrible laugh. Like something breaking.

"Dygall, we're still alive," I said. "We won't be if we lose it, you know? We can't afford to lose it. We just can't."

He blinked at me and swallowed. I think he might have nodded. I'm not sure, though, because at that moment I was distracted by Mum and Arkwright, who had entered the room to look for Yestin's Robo-dog.

"There it is," said Arkwright—but he hesitated. So did Mum. They were studying Yestin.

He didn't seem to notice them until Mum hunkered down in front of him.

"Yestin?" she murmured. "Honey? We need to do something."

My teeth were clenched; I was waiting for the explosion. Yestin was obsessed with that Robo-dog. I was sure that he would never allow anyone to harm it.

But I was wrong. The explosion didn't come. Yestin just gazed blankly, nodding and shrugging, as Mum explained what had to be done. I was wondering if he even understood—if the news was even sinking in—when Dad reappeared.

He began to search through the drawers in the bench.

"What's this?" he asked Sloan, pulling out a long flexible tube.

Sloan flicked a glance at him. "Spare pipe for the hydrolizer."

"And these?"

"I think that's a set of electrodes for plasma arcing."

"What about this?"

"Vacuum valve seal."

"What are you doing, Dad?" I couldn't understand the point of his questions.

It took him a moment to find me down on the floor. When he did, he said, "We need to get hold of a sampler. Firminus and I are trying to devise some sort of trap."

"Oh." That made sense, I supposed. Then Dygall stirred beside me.

"You shouldn't be building traps," he hoarsely remarked. "You should be building *weapons*."

((128))

Dad dropped something at that point, and it broke when it bounced off the bench leg; I heard the tinkling noise. Dad cursed, then stooped to pick up the pieces. It was Sloan who answered Dygall.

"Stop and think," he said quietly, turning his smooth face toward my Little Brother. "If we damage this ship, we'll damage ourselves. We can't treat *Plexus* as an enemy. We have to *help* it, not hurt it. Or we haven't got a chance."

"But—"

"He's right, Dygall." Dad had straightened. "I know it's hard, but we can't let our emotions get the better of us."

"It's all right for *you*," Dygall spat. "You're still—you didn't— my Dad's *dead* . . ." If he hadn't been sedated, he probably would have screamed these words. As it was, he muttered them before moving away from Lais when she tried to hug him.

Meanwhile, Arkwright had picked up Bam. He said, "You might want to do the examination in here, Quenby."

"Yes," said Mum. She rose, pulling Yestin up with her. "You kids, could you go back into the other room, now? It's . . . um . . ."

"Clear," Arkwright finished.

"Yes. It's clear in there." She meant that Zennor's body had been hidden away. In the precision pipe or whatever it was. Before we could move, however, Sloan suddenly said, "There's a high concentration of nitric acid in this toxin sample."

Everyone stared at him. He pointed at a glowing panel on top of his biosensor.

"Check for yourselves," he continued. "It's not the nastiest component, by any means, but it's the largest." When no one had any comment to make, he added, "Which suggests that there might be rather a lot of nitric oxide floating around on this ship somewhere. Unfortunately."

"Nitric oxide?" Mum echoed.

"Correct me if I'm wrong," said Dad, "but isn't nitric acid highly corrosive?" He waved a small metal drum. "I mean, even if we built some sort of suction pump and trapped one of those samplers in this filter canister—"

"It might work its way out," Sloan finished. "Yes."

"Damn."

"But there should be some way of neutralizing the acid," Sloan went on thoughtfully. "I mean, we can *use* the fact that those things are alive. We could start at the molecular level, with something that will inhibit protein synthesis or dissolve peptide bonds. Like interferon, for example. Though we haven't got CAIP to do the cytanalysis, of course—"

"Wait. Wait a second." Mum flapped her left hand at Sloan. Her right hand was clamped across her forehead. "Nitric oxide. *Nitric oxide.*"

We all waited.

"We synthesize our *own* nitric oxide. Every one of us! In our bodies! Peroxide, superoxide, lectoferrin . . ." She counted them off on her fingers. "And nitric oxide! The neutrophils manufacture it to destroy free radicals!"

A few questioning glances were exchanged. Only Sloan seemed to understand what was going on. He stared hard at my mother with narrowed eyes.

"What are neutrophils?" Lais asked cautiously.

"White blood cells! *White blood cells,* Lais!"

Sloan lifted his face and scanned the ceiling. "Those samplers were manufactured to detect impurities," he conceded slowly. "After which they're supposed to signal for a cleanup . . ."

"Wait just a minute." Dad's voice was tight. "Quenby, are you saying—are you saying those samplers are part of the ship's *immune system?*"

I gasped. Once again my mind was flooded with ideas, which came together like chemical reagents sparking other ideas. It all made instant sense. I had studied the immune system at school and remembered how it worked: the first line of defense (skin, mucus, nose hairs), the increase of local temperature (to speed up cell production), the swelling of blood vessels in the brain, the constriction of blood vessels in the skin—and the armies of immune cells. Some of these cells were produced in the bone marrow, some in the lymph nodes. Leukocytes, they were called: white blood cells.

They killed things. Bacteria. Viruses. Foreign bodies of any kind. They were *designed* to kill things.

"But we're not foreign bodies!" I burst out. "We've lived here all our lives!"

"Shh," said Dad. "Don't panic . . ."

"Cheney's right," Sloan agreed, frowning. For the first time he looked worried. "We're like the bacteria in our own gut. We're part of this system; we always have been. How can we have been identified as a threat?"

"Maybe it was me," said Arkwright faintly. He cast his eyes around the room. "I popped that sub-conduit. On the Bridge."

"Oh, but we patched that up." Mum's voice shook. "We fixed it, Arkwright."

"Yes, but suppose someone else didn't?" I had remembered the Remote Access Repair Units. The hydrochloric acid. I spoke before even stopping to think. "Suppose someone saw one of the RARs attacking the struts and threw something at it? There are so many people on board. If just one of us panicked . . ."

I couldn't finish. Sloan was regarding me gravely. Lais had buried her face in her hands. Arkwright swore as Bam wriggled free of his grasp and bounded toward the door.

Before the fleeing Robo-dog even reached it, however, someone cried out. From the other room. Someone who sounded absolutely terrified.

"Oh *no!*" he shouted. "Look! *Oh no!*"

Chapter Twelve

The smell was the first thing we noticed as we poured out of the Pen. It was a terrible smell that made us all cough: a smell of burning meat with another stench overlaying it. Then we saw Firminus standing by the door.

He pointed.

"Something's trying to get in," he rasped.

Where the two fleshy panels met, the door was changing color from pink to brown. Bits of it were sloughing away, in yellow and red streaks. A pale vapor poured off the dissolving tissue.

"Acid," said Sloan.

"But—but it can't be!" This was Lais. "They can't be attacking the fabric of the *ship!*"

"NK cells," Mum croaked.

"What?"

"Natural Killer cells." Mum couldn't take her eyes off the door. Her voice sounded dull. "If there's a virus inhabiting an ordinary cell, an NK cell binds to it and releases chemicals that destroy the cell membrane so that the cell bursts open."

"Holy mother of God," said Ottilie. I froze up. I couldn't think. Natural Killer cells? *Natural Killer cells?*

We didn't stand a chance.

"We have to get out." Dad grabbed my arm. He was scanning the room. "How can we get out?"

"We can't!" Lais wailed.

"Yes, we can."

It was Dygall. He seemed remarkably calm—perhaps because he was still sedated.

"The air ducts," he declared.

The air ducts! Yes! I peered up, searching for the access panel. Because we were on A deck, the air duct ran overhead. It ran between A and B decks, along with the filtration ducts and cable conduit. You could reach it through access panels or through hatches in the stair shafts that could be found at both ends of every street.

"But will the duct be big enough?" somebody wanted to know.

"Oh yes." I knew that. I had spent enough time in Sustainable Services to have learned about the air ducts. "There was a minimum standard circumference set, to allow for manual repair—"

"Come on." Dad jerked me forward. "Kids first."

"No!" about three women exclaimed at once. Then Mum said, "Not in the lead, Tuddor!"

"Sloan, then! Hurry!"

Arkwright had already dragged a stool under the access panel. It didn't look much like an access panel anymore. It had become a semitransparent sheet of membrane streaked with blood vessels.

Arkwright fumbled frantically at its edges, trying to find the release catch.

"For God's sake, Arkwright, hurry *up!*"

"Oh no! Oh no!" Lais was shaking and crying. "Oh *no!*"

"Just *pull* it!" Dygall yelled. "Just rip it off!"

"If I damage it, we won't be able to reseal it," Arkwright replied through his teeth.

"Arkwright, *quickly!*"

"Here." Sloan sprang onto Arkwright's stool, causing Arkwright to lose his balance and fall back onto the floor. Sloan slid his fingers under a flap of muscle above his head. He began to peel open the access panel.

"Someone has to hold it"—he gasped—"while I climb through . . ."

I glanced at the door. Its center was now black. The brown area was getting bigger.

I could hear the hiss of chemical reaction, even through the clamor that everyone was making.

"Go, Sloan, go on!"

"Yestin next!"

"But there are samplers *in* there! *Inside* the air ducts! Aren't there?" This was one of Ottilie's staff. He was in a complete panic. "I'm sure there are! There must be!"

"No," I said, and had to clear my throat. My voice wasn't working properly. "No," I squawked. "Just filters and scrubbers."

"We'll take a chance," Dad said. He released my arm and grabbed Yestin around the waist.

Sloan was already scrambling through the access hole. All I could see of him were his legs. Arkwright was holding the flap back for him.

"You all right, Sloan?" Firminus shouted. He kept glancing from his son to the door.

"Fine!" came the muffled response.

"You next," said Dad, and hoisted Yestin up toward the hole in the ceiling.

"I can't turn around!" Sloan announced. *"It's too narrow!"*

"Grab his feet," Dad ordered. "Yestin? Grab Sloan's feet! He'll pull you in!"

"Will you *hurry?*" Lais screamed.

The black patch on the door was disintegrating; it had been eaten away. There was a hole the size of my fist, and through it I could see . . . something. Something that wasn't pink, like a sampler, but purple. A sort of bluey purple.

Pulsing bluey purple.

"Dad . . ." I faltered.

Dad turned. His expression was hard. "You next," he ordered, reaching for me. But Firminus was already pushing Dygall toward the hole. As Yestin's kicking legs disappeared from sight, Firminus heaved Dygall's unwieldy form toward them.

"Quick!" Firminus grunted. "Grab on . . . !"

"Dad, that's not a sampler. Look!" I could see more of the purple stuff now because the hole was bigger than my head and opening up fast. Through it I could make out streaks of white, a ring of dark polyps, a series of small winking mouths . . . "Dad, it's something else!"

"It's attached itself to the other side of the door," Firminus remarked with a kind of deadly calm. "It's excreting some chemical."

"Just get up there, Cheney!"

I was tall enough to reach the access panel while standing on the stool. When I grabbed the edge of the hatch, it was slippery but yielding. So I was able to dig my fingernails into it. Dad gave me a leg-up.

I remember very clearly my last glimpse of the BioLab—a sweeping view, because I was looking down. I saw a circle of staring eyes and open mouths and sweating faces. I saw Lais cowering under a console. I saw Firminus watching the door, his arms wrapped around his chest, Ottilie standing with her hands locked together over her mouth, one of her staff hefting the magnetron pole. I saw the drooling wound in the door, which was filling the whole room with a horrible stench.

That was all I saw. Dad gave me a huge shove, and I was suddenly in the air duct. In the dark, narrow, slick, circular air duct.

The light in the collar of my pressure suit immediately flicked on. At least its sensor was still working.

"Go! *Go!*" someone screamed from behind me.

I went. I struggled along, using my elbows and toes. (I couldn't get up onto my hands and knees, because the duct was too small.) Ahead I could see Dygall's feet working desperately. The duct wall shuddered with the impact of each kick and nudge.

"I'm here, Cheney!" It was Mum, panting. Gasping for breath. "I'm right behind you! Don't stop!"

I didn't. I couldn't. I thrashed along, gulping down air, sliding, wriggling, until I almost ran my face into the soles of Dygall's boots.

"Go on!" I screamed. "Keep going!"

"Sloan, what are you *doing*?" Dygall cried. I couldn't hear the response. But next thing I knew, we were moving again.

Shortly afterward I passed under a B deck access panel and realized why Sloan had stopped.

Lying across the filter screen was something that looked horribly like an arm. I might have been wrong, of course. It was hard to tell.

Was someone lying on the floor up there? Dead or injured?

"Mum," I said, "there's something overhead . . . through the access panel . . ."

"Keep going."

"It's just—"

"Keep going!"

So I kept going. There wasn't much choice. Whenever I came to another access panel, I would peer through the membrane net, trying to work out our position. I didn't have much luck, though. I could tell when we passed over streets but not which streets they were. The shapes in the compartments were too indistinct to be easily identified. I knew we were heading away from BioLab; that was about it.

I didn't know how many people were behind me. Had we all got out? I didn't have the breath to ask. I almost didn't want to.

At last Dygall came to a halt in front of me. He yelled, in a strained and high-pitched voice, "Sloan says we're at MedLab! The Stasis Banks! Should we stop here?"

I transmitted the message to my mother. Huffing and puffing, she replied, "There are hardly any . . . samplers in the . . . Stasis Banks. It's wall-to-wall . . . pods and their . . . sensors are internal . . ."

"So should we stop?"

"They've got a . . . double pressure . . . seal, too. *And* an air lock filter . . ."

"So should we stop or not? Mum?"

A pause. Then I heard Arkwright's voice, very, very faintly. "We can't stay in here, Quenby. It's not an option."

"No . . ."

"Tell Sloan we'll try the Stasis Banks."

"Did you hear that, Cheney?" asked Mum. "Tell Sloan—"

"I know. I heard."

I passed on the message. Within seconds the duct began to shake as, somewhere up ahead, Sloan thumped at an access panel. It took him a while to break through. I heard Dygall say "Yuck!" and wondered what vessel Sloan might have ruptured in the ship's fabric.

"Quenby!" It was Arkwright again. I could hardly understand him; his words were muffled by my mother's intervening body. "Don't let those kids climb down first! Tell them to keep going, over the panel, and then they can back up once I'm down!"

"Good idea," Mum said. "Cheney—"

"Yeah. I heard." Once more I transmitted the message. Sloan, however, ignored it; I don't think he considered himself a "kid." Dygall ignored it, too. He often ignored suggestions. Only Yestin did as he was told.

Suddenly I found myself on the edge of a void. Below me two faces were staring up out of the dimness.

One of them was Sloan's.

"Don't worry," he said. "Just crawl across the hole until your legs have drop space. I'll catch you. It's not a big fall."

It wasn't, either. Despite Mum's protests I swung myself through the hole until I was dangling from the ceiling like an old-fashioned pendant light. "There are no samplers, Quenby!" Sloan declared as he reached for my waist.

Dygall was sitting on the floor with his head in his hands. The floor itself was so soft that, if I *had* come down hard, I would have been cushioned.

Sloan caught me, though. He let me down gently.

I looked around.

"It's so dark," I croaked.

"It's always dark in the Vaults," Sloan replied, using our nickname for the Stasis Banks. "You know that. Hey, Quenby! I'll catch you!"

I had never liked this area of the ship. Not that I had been in it very often; you had to have special clearance. But I had visited the Vaults once or twice for school and had found the long racks of pods rather creepy. Everyone in those pods looked so *dead*— though they weren't, of course. They were in cytopic suspension, being monitored carefully by all the sensors hooked up to them. You could see them through the clear silicon casings, face after face, form after form, like the statues lined up along a particular corridor in our mimexic tour of Ancient Rome.

I'd always had the sense that one of those motionless figures was going to open his or her eyes as I trudged past. Even though I knew it was impossible. No one just snaps out of cytopic suspension. It takes a long time and a lot of careful adjustments. If it's not done with absolute precision, you can get badly hurt.

Surveying the silent ranks of B Crew stretching for a long, long way in both directions, I suddenly thought, *Something's wrong.*

They didn't look normal.

"Ooof!" said Mum. She had come down a little too fast and had fallen to her knees. But she quickly struggled to her feet again. "Cheney? Are you okay?"

"Mum, look." Nervously I edged toward the nearest pod. The beam of light from my collar-spot hit the pod's casing, which was no longer a clear, glassy silicon but something softer and more cloudy. It looked almost as if it would wobble if you touched it. Nevertheless, despite this change my light-beam did manage to penetrate the casing and illuminate what lay beneath.

There was still a person inside, who seemed to be disappearing into a kind of pink jelly. The tube inserted under his skin, near his collarbone, was now the same color as the skin itself. The trodes on his body were sending out shoots, weaving a fine web across his head and limbs and torso. One of the filaments had even worked its way into the corner of an eye . . .

"Don't look!" Mum snapped. She jerked me away. "Don't look."

"Oh . . . oh no . . ."

"We can't help them, Cheney. Don't look."

It was too late. I had seen, and felt sick. I had to take big breaths. "They're connected to CAIP." I groaned. "They're part of the ship now . . ."

"Shh!"

It was like a nightmare. It was the sort of thing only the sickest of minds could ever have imagined. But there was worse to come.

Yestin had slid down from the ceiling. Arkwright had followed him and now stood dragging his fingers through his sticky hair, his chest laboring as he shook his head at Sloan. Arkwright's knees were shaking. His expression was blank.

Sloan frowned. He squinted up at the access panel. His collarspot wavered over the dark, gaping hole above him.

"Where's Dad?" I whispered. "Where are the others?"

But I already knew the answer. I could sense it from the way Arkwright winced and closed his eyes.

The others weren't with us.

Chapter Thirteen

It was Sloan who finally found the words. I was speechless. "What happened?" he asked.

"Tuddor sealed the panel," Arkwright replied hoarsely.

"Behind you?"

"I didn't . . ." Arkwright paused, took a deep breath, then turned his huge bloodshot eyes toward my mother. "There were samplers coming in," he explained, choosing his words with an obvious effort. "Samplers and those blue—I mean, those scent pellet things. I'm sorry, Quenby. I didn't know. Not until . . . It was Tuddor who made the decision."

Someone patted my arm, but I didn't even look around.

"What happened to my dad?"

"Cheney, I'm sorry. I don't know—"

"They got him!"

"No—"

"They did!"

"I don't know. I didn't see."

"You did see!" I could tell from his face. It looked bruised. When I stepped forward, Sloan grabbed me.

"What happened, Arkwright?" my mother demanded. She spoke very quietly. "You'd better tell us."

Arkwright hesitated, and I felt as if my chest were going to burst open. Sloan was still holding my arm. Dygall hovered at my side. Yestin was behind me—I wasn't sure where.

I could barely stand up, let alone keep track of Yestin.

"One of the samplers got Lais." Arkwright sighed at long last. We all waited, mute with shock.

"It went straight past Tuddor and attacked Lais. The last thing I saw was Ottilie getting hit by a scent pellet. That was the *last thing I saw.*"

"But they should have come after us." Dygall had finally found his voice. "Why didn't the others follow us? Tuddor and Firminus and the rest?"

"No time," said Arkwright. "They had to seal the air duct before any samplers got in."

"But—"

"When I last saw Tuddor, he was alive. Firminus, too," Arkwright added.

"If they were alive, they would have come after us!" I gasped, and Mum suddenly seemed to snap out of her daze. As Sloan fell back, she came up and put her arms around me.

"It's all right," she said, as if she were trying to convince herself. I could feel her shaking. "Dad's smart. Dad's very smart. He'll think of something. He will."

"That's right," Dygall agreed faintly. "He—he could have got out while the samplers were attacking someone else. He could have."

"He had to seal up the duct, Cheney." Yestin's contribution was low and lifeless. "Maybe he had to get out of BioLab before he had a chance to *unseal* it. Maybe he's hiding somewhere."

Sloan said nothing. I was staring over my mum's shoulder, straight at his angular profile. His dark eyes were narrowed. He looked very pale.

"Listen," said Arkwright. "There's every chance they're still alive, because these attacks *aren't random*." Failing to get any response from me or my mother, he addressed Sloan. "That thing *targeted* Lais. It went straight past Tuddor. Why?"

"Because Lais was marked," Sloan volunteered after a moment.

"*Exactly*. Lais was *marked*. So was Zennor. Both of them. The blue tag—"

"And Ottilie, too," Sloan murmured.

"Yes." Arkwright paused. "I—I don't hold out much hope for Ottilie."

"Antibodies," Sloan continued slowly and thoughtfully. "They're like antibodies. Antibodies are markers. Each has evolved to recognize a particular virus. They lock on to its spikes so the virus can't clone itself. And they mark it for destruction."

"Oh my God," Mum breathed into my neck. She squeezed me hard.

Dygall spoke up beside me. "Are you saying . . . Do you mean that the samplers won't hit you unless a scent pellet hits you first?" he asked Sloan.

"It makes sense. Scent pellets and samplers. Antibodies and T cells."

"It would explain why so many of these . . . these *entities* seem to ignore us," said Arkwright in a slightly distracted tone. "What if there's only a single scent-pellet antibody for each person on board? Or just a few of them, perhaps?"

"You mean there's something out there with *my name on it?*" Dygall screeched.

"Shh," said Yestin, flinching.

But Sloan shrugged. "Looks like it," he conceded.

"And we've got to ask ourselves: what's the recognition factor?" Arkwright surveyed our huddled group, his hands on his hips. "How do they pinpoint their targets? Where does the information come from? What allows them to match their target specifications with our personal details?"

There was a long pause. At first I didn't understand what he was getting at. My brain wasn't working very well at the time; I was still fighting back the urge to scream and wail and fall on the floor crying out for my dad. Mum, too, was not at her best. Dygall hadn't fully recovered, either.

It was Sloan who lifted his wrist suddenly and stared at his ID band. Then he looked at Arkwright, wide-eyed.

"Signal codes," he said, and Arkwright nodded gravely.

"That's what I think."

"The wristbands!"

"What else?"

"We have to get them off," said Yestin. He had snapped out of his stupor; something appeared to have clicked in his head. "Quick!" he exclaimed. "Before they find us!" And he began to gnaw at his own wristband.

It was a futile attempt—as Mum knew full well. "Yestin," she protested, "don't do that. It's pointless . . ."

"It's too tough for teeth," Arkwright agreed. "It has to be cut. Have you got anything, Quenby?"

"Who, me?" Mum stared at him in utter confusion. I knew just how she felt.

"Didn't you bring your Medkit?" Sloan asked.

"My *Medkit?*"

"Of course she didn't!" Dygall snapped. "She didn't have time!"

"What about you?" Sloan turned to Arkwright. "Don't you have an atomic screwdriver, or something?"

Arkwright shook his head. He glanced around at the dim expanses of the Stasis Banks as if hoping that something sharp might materialize out of the shadows. But there wasn't an edge left in the whole place. It was all doughy soft tissue and slimy surfaces.

Sloan remarked, "There are two sides to this, you know. Those samplers need our wristbands to target us, but they also need our details on file. If we could get into CAIP and wipe those files—"

"Yes, well, we can't just now," Arkwright retorted. Then Mum took a deep breath and pointed out that we weren't far from the Infirmary. There were plenty of penetrating instruments in there, she said.

"If we go through the two pressure-seal doors at the end of this compartment, we'll get into the next cell." Mum sounded as if she was drained of all energy. "The Infirmary's over there," she added.

"But what if the samplers are, too?" Dygall was haranguing us; his voice seemed to grate on my ears. "What if we open the doors, and they all come flying in? They'll get us then! We won't have a hope!"

Again there was silence. Mum's grip on me had slackened; we were still entwined, but loosely. My mind was just starting to tick over again. I thought, *Pressure seal. Double doors. Air lock filter.* Sloan, however, jumped in ahead of me.

"Are you saying it's an air lock filter through there? With two pressure doors?" he asked my mother.

"That's right."

"So even if those things start eating their way through, it's going to take them twice as long?"

"I—I guess so."

"Well, then—why don't you people stay while I use the air duct?" Sloan squinted up at the access panel. "I'll try to get into the Infirmary that way. Pick up a few laser probes or molecule displacement scalpels and bring them back."

"Oh no." My mother stiffened. I caught my breath. Even Yestin gave a squeak of protest. But Sloan wasn't going to listen to us.

"It's the best solution," he insisted before we could say anything further. "It puts only one of us at risk. If I don't like the look of the Infirmary, I can always move on. Or come straight back."

"But we shouldn't split up!" Mum demurred.

"We must. What other option do we have?"

"Just one," said Arkwright, pulling at his pointed chin. "I'll go."

"No."

"It's not your decision, Sloan." Arkwright used the same detached tone I'd often heard him employ when he was trying to pull me out of a circuitry quagmire during our training sessions together. "I outrank you. It's my decision."

"Then use your head," said Sloan with equal calm. "You're not expendable. I am."

"Sloan!" Mum exclaimed, and I cried, "That's not true!"

"Of course it's true." Sloan flicked me an impatient glance. "We all are, to some degree, except Quenby and Arkwright. They're the only ones with enough expertise to solve our main problem—which is getting into CAIP. Arkwright, especially. You can't risk yourself, Arkwright. It wouldn't be logical."

Arkwright blinked. He seemed taken aback. As he searched for an answer, Mum said, "Your father wouldn't allow it, Sloan."

Sloan turned his head in a deliberate fashion. I couldn't see the expression in his eyes. It was too dark. But his voice, when he spoke, was hard and cool.

"Since my father isn't here—and is in fact very probably dead—his opinion isn't relevant. So let's just forget about my father and concentrate on the matter at hand. Which, let's face it, is the preservation of our entire species."

We were stunned. Even Arkwright couldn't find the words. I didn't know how to feel. I was both appalled and impressed. Dygall gaped. Mum seemed to shrink. Yestin swallowed audibly.

When Sloan spoke again, after regarding us silently for a few seconds, he emphasized his point with just a few incisive phrases.

"If we're going to survive, we're going to have to start thinking clearly," he announced. "This is a matter of *survival*. There's no room here for fussing or fuming, or worrying about inessentials. About other people's feelings." He addressed Arkwright. "Now give me a leg-up," he ordered, "and I'll be back in a few minutes."

Arkwright obeyed. Sheepishly he heaved Sloan back into the air duct. I stood there catching my breath; it was as if someone had just thrown a bucket of cold water in my face. For a short while nobody said anything. The only sound was a series of squeaks and rustles as Sloan's feet disappeared from sight.

We could watch his progress in the air duct, because both it and the ceiling were now constructed of slightly elastic material. The bulges made by the pressure of his hands and knees were clearly visible as he crawled away from us. Naturally we tried to stay beneath him, plotting his course until he passed over the first pressure door. Then we had to stop, releasing a collective sigh.

With trembling fingers Dygall prodded the door—which was no longer so much a door as a giant valve.

"This looks okay," he muttered. "It's not even hot. I don't think anything's reached it, yet."

"But something's bound to come soon." I shivered, thinking about the BioLab door. And my dad too, of course. "Don't—don't you think we should disable the pressure pad?"

"With what?" Dygall's voice cracked. He sounded ready to explode. "We don't have a magnetron pole."

"Disable anything and it might alert CAIP," Arkwright warned, at which point Mum reached out and patted Dygall's shoulder.

"We'll be safe once we've cut off these bands," she assured him. No doubt she was simply trying to comfort the children—this, I knew, was how her mind worked—but her simple remark had an unexpected consequence.

Because Yestin, who was also fingering the door, suddenly asked, "Why will we be safe?" When he received no immediate reply, he swung around to stare at Mum. "Why *should* we be safe, Quenby?"

"Well—ah . . ." Mum struggled to provide a satisfactory answer. I was holding her hand, and I squeezed it. "Well, as Arkwright said, we—our ID bands provide targets—"

"Yes, but why go to all that bother?" Yestin now fixed his round greenish eyes on Arkwright. He was genuinely puzzled. I knew the signs. "It would be easy enough to kill us without attacking doors," he said. "You could shut down the photosynthesis machines. Or stop dispensing food. Why doesn't the ship do that?"

It was a good question. It was a *very* good question. And I couldn't believe that I hadn't considered it before. Too much else happening, perhaps.

"He's right," said Dygall, and fixed Arkwright with an accusing glare. "How come we can still breathe and eat?"

"Maybe—maybe the oxygen just hasn't run out yet." I hardly

liked to say it, but it had to be said. "With so many people dead maybe it would take longer than normal . . ."

Mum made a strangled noise. But Arkwright shook his head, frowning at the floor. "No," he said, dismissing my suggestion with a flick of his fingers. "No, because what about the gravitational pitch? That's still normal. There's been no depressurization. The *lights* are still on. Why are the lights still on? Why let us see? The samplers don't need to see. The Remote Access Units don't have eyes; they have sensors." He looked up. "Yestin's right. He's nailed it. Those lights are for our benefit. So is the air quality. So are the rotation stabilizers and the food dispensers. In which case, why haven't they been turned off?"

Was it a rhetorical question? I glanced at Mum. Yestin glanced at me. We were lost.

"It's *obvious,*" Arkwright went on impatiently. "If the ship's trying to get rid of us, why keep the systems running?"

I cleared my throat. "Because . . . because the ship needs them, too?" I proposed tentatively.

"*Correct.*" It was turning into another training session. "Because the ship needs them, too."

"But why?" Mum leaned forward. "Why would anything *living* need lights inside it?"

"Because of the cooling system," I cried. Suddenly I understood. It made sense. All the endless training I'd done in Sustainable Services, about balance and seamless systems and sustainability and carbon cycles—at last it had paid off. "The cooling system's adjusted to neutralize the extra heat produced by the lighting system!" I went on, thinking aloud.

"Precisely," said Arkwright.

"And the microbe populations were engineered to survive at normal temperature, in an exactly calibrated level of ambient light—"

"*Yes.*" Arkwright thrust his face into my mother's—he had a tendency to intrude on people's personal space when he got excited. "This ship was as complex as any living organism even before we hit that emission wave. Fiddle with its systems, and you throw the whole balance out of whack."

"So whatever was normal before—" I began.

". . . stays normal," Arkwright finished, and Dygall gave a bark of wild, scornful laughter.

"You call this *normal?*" he squawked, whereupon Arkwright regarded him with a grave look.

"On a scale of one to ten? Yes, I would describe this situation as falling on the normal side of the median point," he responded. "Just think—we could all be floating around in goo by now. In total darkness."

"But we're under *attack!*" Dygall exclaimed fiercely.

"Yes, we are. And I think Cheney was right. I think we're under attack because someone, somewhere, stepped over the line. I think CAIP is trying to restore this ship to a condition of normalcy—that is, to a condition as close as possible to the way it was when it passed through that emission wave. To do it, CAIP must wipe out the threat of anyone smashing up a Remote Access Unit or whatever it was that happened to trigger this immune response."

Mum was gnawing at her bottom lip. "So our best hope is—?"

"Our best hope is to do what Sloan suggested. Get into CAIP, wipe all the personnel files, and CAIP won't know what to look for."

"But—but . . ." Yestin's voice shook. He was using the door to steady himself. "But can't we—I mean—can't we go back to the way it was before?" he pleaded. "I mean, isn't *that* our best hope?"

I suppose, in a way, he spoke for all of us. All of us must have been nursing the expectation, deep in our hearts, that we would somehow reverse the process we'd been witnessing. After all, this was a ship. It wasn't a great big space-borne jellyfish, or a mollusk, or any other kind of multicellular life form. It was a *ship*. It was *our* ship.

Surely we could take charge and restore it to its former condition?

That's what we all wanted. But it wasn't going to happen. I knew it wasn't, even as I turned to look at Arkwright, anxious to hear his reply.

He hesitated before delivering his final verdict. It was Yestin, after all, who had asked the question: pale, fragile Yestin, with his deformed joints and pinched face and skinny legs. Only the most heartless person could have smashed Yestin's feeble hopes without a qualm.

"You know," said Arkwright, "I've never been a religious man, Yestin, but what's happened here—well, you could almost call it a miracle of sorts. We've witnessed the creation of life. It's something quite beyond our capabilities, even now." Arkwright took a deep breath. "And quite frankly, if you want my honest opinion," he continued, "it would take a second miracle to cancel out the first."

His long face grew longer as Yestin dropped his gaze and covered his mouth.

"I'm sorry," Arkwright finished. "I do think we have a chance, I really do. But I don't think it involves a life that will be anything like our old one."

Chapter Fourteen

Sloan returned soon afterward. It was Yestin who first spotted the bulges in the ceiling. When Arkwright yelled, "Sloan? Is that you?" we all heard a faint but unmistakable reply.

So we hurried to the access hole, where we awaited Sloan's reappearance.

After a while his face popped into view, illuminated from below by his collar-spot. He was breathing heavily.

"Are you all right?" Mum demanded.

A nod. Then his face disappeared for an instant, to be replaced by his flapping legs. Arkwright caught them but was kicked out of the way. Sloan preferred to jump down unaided.

"Floor's so soft," he explained, after hitting it. "You don't need help."

"Well?" said Dygall, who had never been one to mince his words. "What happened? What have you got?"

"Laser-head scalpel," Sloan replied, fumbling in his pocket.

"Is that *all?*"

Sloan looked at him. Mum said quickly, "That's fine. We'll use that."

"Given time," Sloan remarked, raising one eyebrow, "I could probably have found more."

"But you had to get back," Mum concluded. "Exactly." She relieved Sloan of the laser-head, switched it on, and set its frequency. It sliced through her wristband like a knife through soft butter. "Who's next? Cheney? Careful, now."

One by one we had our ID bands removed. Cradling his, Arkwright observed, "These things are heat-powered, aren't they?"

"Yes," said Mum. She was hunched over Yestin's arm, wielding her scalpel with great concentration. "They'll stop working soon if they're not placed next to a heat source with the correct output."

"Then we'll leave them here," Arkwright decided. He dropped his band on the floor. Dygall followed suit. He even ground it under his heel for good measure.

"So what's the situation over there?" Arkwright asked Sloan. "Any samplers?"

"One or two." Sloan pulled back his hand as my mother reached for it. He had already cut off his own ID band. "I'd forgotten that those pressure doors open into the surgical theater—"

"In case something happens to one of B Crew," Mum interjected. "It means a fast transference."

"Right. Well, I only had to duck into the theater. Plenty of stuff to choose from. The door to Pathology was open, but I couldn't see much activity. One or two samplers. One scent pellet. They didn't bother me. I didn't check the Infirmary. I would have had to cross the street to do that."

"What about—?" my mother began, then stopped. I knew what she wanted to ask. We probably all did. It was Yestin who finally found the courage.

"Was anyone else there?" he queried in a very small voice.

Sloan didn't reply immediately. He rubbed his wrist where the ID band had been. At last he said, without lifting his gaze from the floor, "I saw two people."

"You *did?*" cried Mum.

"They were dead, though."

"Oh." My mother returned the laser-head to him.

"We have morgue facilities somewhere, don't we, Quenby?" Sloan continued in a matter-of-fact tone. "Body bags and such?"

"Yes, but . . . they're on the other side of MedLab. A few streets down." Mum swallowed. "Did you see who they . . . I mean, did you recognize them?"

"I recognized one of them."

We waited. Suddenly Sloan turned on his heel and threw back his head. He was eyeing the access hole. "It was my mother," he declared flatly. "Arkwright, could you give me a leg-up?"

But Arkwright just stood frozen to the spot. Mum covered her mouth with one hand. I felt the tears well in my eyes.

I couldn't stand it. I just couldn't stand it anymore.

"Oh my dear," said Mum. "I'm so sorry . . ."

"It wasn't entirely unexpected." Sloan seemed more irritable than anything else. "Arkwright! Could you help me, here? Time is of the essence."

"Yes, I—yes, of course." Arkwright stepped forward. Then he frowned. "Wait," he said. "Where are you going?"

"Back to MedLab. It's a good spot. Good facilities. Pathology's almost as well equipped as BioLab. And there's a food dispenser." But nobody moved, and Sloan looked around, grim-faced. "Well?" he demanded. "What's wrong? Has anyone got a better idea?"

Nobody did. I suppose the rest of us were a long way behind Sloan. So much had happened that I, for one, had not caught up with it all. Zennor. Dad. And now Sloan . . . Poor Sloan. And Sadira. At least I wasn't *sure* that Dad was dead. There was a slim chance that he might be alive. Especially if he'd removed his ID band.

We couldn't be the *only* ones who had worked that out.

"We have to warn people," I said hoarsely. "About the ID bands. We have to spread the word somehow."

Sloan nodded. When he replied, however, his response was "First things first, Cheney."

"But it's important!"

"I know. The trouble is we might be wrong. We can't go waltzing off to warn the others without testing our theory about these wristbands. Not without some kind of protection."

"That's right!" Dygall agreed.

"Nothing explosive or electrical," Sloan went on. "Nothing that will damage the hull or upset the biosystem. Something localized—a chemical might do the trick. There are plenty of chemicals to choose from around MedLab, and there's at least one Interface Array for Arkwright to work with. If *Plexus* is alive, what better place to get a handle on its inner workings than MedLab?" He waved his hand. "We're certainly not going to achieve anything productive by staying *here*."

He was right. We had to do something constructive. People *had* to be warned. As I stood awaiting my turn for a leg-up, I tried to focus on the problem at hand—to ignore my whirling head and churning stomach. The trick was to think about other things. To distract myself. To put my feelings in a box and lock it, the way Sloan had. Sloan was setting a good example. If we fell apart now, we were lost. We had to *think,* and we had to *plan,* and we had to put our hysteria aside until there was time enough to deal with it.

Communication was the key. While Arkwright focused on CAIP and Mum helped him to master its neural networks, I would try to spread the word. Somehow. Without the use of a comm-link.

"Arkwright?" I said.

He grunted. Then, with a heave, he pushed my mother into the air duct.

"What?" he gasped, dodging her flailing boot.

"I was just thinking . . . If the lights are on, and the air's fine, and the gravitational pull is constant . . ."

"Yes?"

"I just wondered—why isn't the Audio Interlink Network up and running?"

I was last in line, bar one. Arkwright had laced his fingers together in preparation for my departure. Now he paused in the act of stooping.

"Good question," he said.

"It's not normal, is it? It's not doing what it used to do."

"No. But then, you have to consider the structural shift at a subatomic level. What we had here before was a very carefully worked-out transmission matrix, with a lot of highly conductive metals involved." He scratched his head, glancing around at the moist, spongy surfaces that enclosed us. "Now we've got a whole ship made of . . . well, I don't know, exactly, but it's organic, and it must have *some* properties unsympathetic to our matrix. Perhaps it's a better insulator than it is a conductor."

"Then how come the scent pellets can track us down? They must have been picking up emission waves from our ID bands—"

"From a short distance, Cheney. We don't know about long distances. If they could pick up our signatures from far away, we'd probably all be dead by now. As it is, they seem to be just wandering around until they bump into us. Or that's the way *I* see it." Arkwright laced his fingers together again. "Come on. Up you go."

I went. The crawl to MedLab wasn't long; it took only a few minutes. When I arrived at the correct access panel, Sloan was waiting for me down below. He grabbed me as I dropped, and held me up as my eyes adjusted to the bright light. Then he nudged me aside to make way for Arkwright.

Blinking, I peered around. We were standing in the surgical theater, which was a compartment that could not be reached from the street. Instead, access was through Pathology (which was right next door) or through the Stasis Banks (which occupied the adjoining pressure cell). I wasn't very familiar with the theater—or with Pathology. Even if I had been, I might not have recognized either room. They were like a pair of lungs now: two bags of air surrounded by springy tissue. You practically bounced with each step. Hatches and storage cupboards lurked somewhere beneath a web of glistening fibers and dense, dark, purple swellings. In the midst of all the strangely shaped nodules that had once been chairs or monitors or surgical tables, the remaining furniture looked very odd. There were a couple of wheeled cabinets, and some gas cylinders, and a stand with various bits of equipment hanging off it.

That stand was being used to prop open the door—or valve—between Pathology and the theater. Mum had already passed through the gap; I could see her standing over a slumped and lifeless shape in the next room. Dygall was with her.

I recognized the smell that hung in the air. I also recognized the thick, luxurious black hair on the body that my mother was surveying.

I didn't want to look too closely. Instead I turned to help Arkwright, who had hit the floor behind me.

"I'm okay," he said, recovering his balance. "Where's Quenby?"

"In there." Yestin pointed.

"Ah."

"This place is no good!" Dygall called to us from the next room. "The door's been burned through out here! You can see straight into the street!"

"Come back, then," said Arkwright. "This communicating door seems to be intact."

"What about . . . ?" Dygall gestured at Sadira's remains.

"We'll deal with that later. Just come back in."

Arkwright was nervous. So was I. I felt exposed, despite the fact that I was no longer wearing an ID band. As Mum and Dygall retraced their steps, Arkwright said, "Who propped open this door, anyway?"

"Not me," said Sloan. "It was like that when I first arrived."

"Ah."

"So we'd better not take the stand away unless we absolutely have to," Sloan added. "Or we might not be able to get it open again."

"I'm so thirsty." Yestin was leaning against a wall. His voice was a mere thread of sound. "Hungry, too . . ."

"Well, first thing we do is feed ourselves," said Sloan. "Then Cheney and I can concentrate on weapons while Arkwright and Quenby look into accessing CAIP—"

"What about me?" Dygall interrupted in a high, hard tone. "I want to concentrate on weapons, too."

"Fine. Whatever." Sloan waved his hand. "Once we have weapons, we can start some reconnaissance sweeps . . . try to pass the word about those wristbands . . ."

"Do we even need weapons if we don't have wristbands?" Mum inquired, and Sloan shrugged.

"You tell me. Personally I'd rather be safe than sorry."

"So . . . hang on." I couldn't get things straight. I put my hands to my head. "What are we doing?"

"I need some kind of neural map," Arkwright announced. He had moved over to the theater Interface Array, which was still vaguely recognizable, though the console was all pulsing lumps and the plasma had turned pink. "I need to superimpose a neural map on the circuitry network," he said, "and then I might know what I'm doing. Quenby?"

"A map's all very well, but there's still the question of access." Mum joined Arkwright at the Array, wringing her hands. "I've been thinking. Immune cells release cytokines. Cytokines are communicator proteins, which determine immune response type. There's even one class of cytokine—it's called chemokine—that's responsible for the actual *positioning* of immune cells. Perhaps if we could inhibit the production of chemokines somehow . . ."

Sloan poked me. When I glanced at him, he jerked his head.

"Come on," he murmured.

"Huh?"

"They're on it. They're busy. Let's see what we can find out here."

I stared at Sloan, who was speaking and moving more quickly than usual. Apart from that, he seemed virtually unaffected by our situation. His dark hair was ruffled, his neck was scratched (how?), but he didn't seem upset. He didn't seem aware that his dead mother lay just a few meters away.

I couldn't understand him. I admired him, I was even in awe of him, but I couldn't understand him.

Dumbly, I followed him into Pathology, which was a larger room than the theater. Most of it now sagged and quivered when touched, but there were a few items that had not been affected. Sloan headed straight for a set of canisters stacked to our right, opposite the door to the street.

I edged around Sadira's body, carefully averting my eyes. The smell made me hold my breath. Through the ragged gap in the outer door, I caught a glimpse of the street, and of a leg sprawled across it. From where I stood, I couldn't see exactly what the leg was attached to—but I *could* see something that made me jump.

The leg was twitching.

"Sloan!" I squeaked. "Look!"

"I know." He was checking the canisters, discarding them one by one with a disappointed hiss. "Somebody's dead. I saw."

"No—it's *moving!*"

"What?" He spoke sharply. He probably turned around; I'm not sure, because I was edging toward the burned hole. With each step my view of the leg improved. The limb was attached to a torso, and the torso was twitching, too. I carefully craned my neck until I was positioned well enough to see the top half of the person outside—then pulled back abruptly, slamming my head into Sloan's chin.

"Ow!"

I couldn't apologize. I could only retch. Dygall reached me as Sloan pushed past, anxious to see what I had just seen. Yestin had also followed us into Pathology; he watched Dygall grab my arm.

"What is it?" Dygall hissed. "Cheney?"

"Shh!"

"What's the matter?"

"Good God," breathed Sloan. One look was enough for him. He stumbled away from the opening, flapping his hands at us. "Back!" he whispered. "Get back!"

"What—"

"There's something out there!" Sloan's voice was barely audible as he shooed us across the room. Dygall tried to resist.

"What do you mean, 'something'?" he demanded.

"It looks like—could it be an *OTV*? Cheney?"

"I—I think so." It certainly resembled an On-board Transport Vehicle. It was the right size, the right shape, and the right color: a charcoal gray capsule as big as a standard single bedroom, with a thin red strip along its flank. It had retained the little black shield on its nose, and the hand-grip shafts next to each door. But the shafts were now whipping around like tentacles; the vast expanse of tinted glass was now part of a slimy, fibrous envelope; and the doors were now wrapped around . . . around . . .

"It's eating," I groaned. "It's out there *eating someone.*"

Chapter Fifteen

"He was already dead," Sloan hissed. "He was. I saw him earlier. That thing wasn't around, then . . ."

"We'd better get back." Yestin tugged at my sleeve frantically. "Let's get back in the air duct. *Now!* Before it sees us!"

"Wait." Sloan was watching the hole in the door. "It probably *can't* see us. Not without our wristbands."

"Sloan—"

"I know. Don't take risks. But there's a bunch of pressure flasks over there. I need to find out what's inside."

"*Sloan!*" I couldn't believe it. "Do you want to get *eaten? Don't be a fool!*"

"We have to get back in the theater!" Yestin pleaded under his breath. "Now!"

"Just wait," Sloan rejoined quietly. "Just get in the theater and wait. I can use my laser-head if things get nasty."

"Against *that?*" I squeaked. "It's *enormous!*"

"Exactly. It's far too big to get through the hole."

"Sloan—"

"I won't be a second."

And he bolted across the room toward the vacuum flasks. I pursued him, of course. It never occurred to me that I shouldn't. Dygall came, too—but not Yestin. He dashed back to alert Mum.

I was furious. I didn't want my mother out there.

"Yestin!" I whispered. "Don't—damn it!"

"Nothing," growled Sloan. The label on the flask in his hand was signaling EMPTY; there was nothing on it except a pressure reading. The flask that I picked up was the same. Together we scrabbled through the remaining flasks, glancing over our shoulders every so often while Dygall passed behind us. He was heading for the dispenser, which lay on the far side of the room.

"Get back, Dygall!" I was so angry, I found it hard to keep my voice down. "You idiot!"

"We need food!"

"Dygall!" I reared up and scurried over to him. "Leave it! Come on!"

"Let go!"

"It's probably like a macrophage of some kind," Sloan murmured distractedly. "They're scavenger cells . . ."

Then several things happened at once. As my furious mother appeared at the communicating door, something charged through the other door—the door to the street. An eruption of fluid was accompanied by a horrible tearing sound, and there it was suddenly. Between me and the theater. The OTV.

It was like something you would normally see through a microscope. Its cylindrical body bobbed about in a fluid kind of way, and through the pulsing, wallowing, charcoal gray walls of muscle I could vaguely make out pale, heavy shapes that might have been (God, it was awful) the limp remains of its latest meal. Its tentacles lashed about, and its doors—one on each side—opened and shut like the mouth of a sea anemone.

I couldn't believe how big it was, even in that big room. It had torn a huge hole in the wall and was squirming around in the yellow goo now spurting from all the damaged vessels. I don't know where its eyes were, but it could see. Or sense. Because it headed straight for Sloan, who was standing right in front of it.

He dodged away. Though it was quick, it wasn't quick enough. Sloan sprang aside and hurled himself through the theater door, which snapped shut as he knocked down the stand that was holding it open. I saw all this in the split second it took me to grab a handful of Dygall's suit. I didn't think. I just moved. I made for the ragged, bleeding gash that the OTV had left behind. In other words, I made for the street. Screaming.

If the OTV had been quicker—as quick as a sampler, for instance—I wouldn't be alive now. Perhaps all the corpses in its belly had slowed it down. Whatever the reason, we got out, Dygall and I. We scrambled into the street and ran, ran for our lives, without the faintest idea of where we were going. We were so stupid. So lucky. For all we knew, there was another OTV just around the next corner. It never even crossed my mind that we could have been running into a nest of OTVs. I never stopped to think, *Oh! Does this mean that the samplers can target us even without our wristbands, or is it just the OTVs?* I simply ran like an animal, up one street, sharp right at the tube, slipping and sliding and stumbling along until I reached the next street. Down that one. Left at the intersection. And left again . . .

Then I was pulled back. Dygall had dug in his heels.

He was pointing. "There!" he gasped. "Air duct!"

The air ducts. Of course. We had to get into an air duct.

Dygall was pointing at a damaged door. Through it I could see a room as black as a scab—its walls bulging with all kinds of strange flaps and knots and protrusions—which was empty save for a large metal toolbox.

Dygall pounced on the toolbox.

"Quick!" he shrieked, dragging it under the access panel.

After a moment my vision cleared and I joined him. I jumped up on the toolbox, but I still couldn't reach the panel.

"Here! Quick!" I crouched down. "Stand on my back!"

He managed it, somehow. Once he slipped and nearly ripped my ear off, but I was past caring. We were both sobbing for breath, sweating and staring and incoherent. Dygall tore the access panel free with clawing fingernails, doing it some damage. Hot, white fluid dripped onto my neck. Blood dripped onto my knee from my torn ear.

"Quick!" he shrilled. "Help me! *Help me!*"

I gave him a boost, springing to my feet so that he was thrust upward. Once he was inside, he backed over the hole, wriggling and scrabbling until he was able to lean out, extending his arms. I must have climbed them somehow. I certainly gave his shoulder socket a nasty yank; it troubled him for a long time afterward.

I don't really remember, to tell you the truth. I was too frantic.

All I remember is the sense of relief when we were finally huddled in that stuffy, dingy, enclosed tube.

"Can you seal it?" Dygall spluttered from behind me. "Can you close up the panel?"

"I—I—"

"You've *got* to, Cheney, *quick!*"

"I know, I know . . ." The panel didn't exactly snap back together—not the way it was supposed to—but I managed. The leaking fluid was already tacky, coagulating like blood; I was able to use it as a kind of glue. We waited for a few minutes, until it had almost dried. Until it was safe to crawl over.

While we were waiting, Dygall said, "They'll be in an air duct, too, don't you think? Arkwright and—"

"Yes."

"That door closed, didn't it? The one to the theater?"

"Yes."

"They would have had time to make it back into the air duct."

"Oh yes."

"Cheney . . ." His voice broke on a sob. He began to sniff and choke.

I couldn't do anything for him. I was beyond tears, and couldn't think of a single comforting thing to say except, "They've probably gone back to the Vaults."

There was a long pause. At last Dygall said thickly, "Do you know which direction?"

"I—uh . . ." It was hard to concentrate. Which way had we been running? The escape had slipped by in a panic-stricken blur.

"I—I think the other way," Dygall rasped.

"I think you're right." Reviewing our route in my mind, I added, "There should be a junction up ahead. Over the street. We should turn left there."

"Cheney?"

"What?"

"It saw us." Dygall was speaking very, very quietly, and I didn't blame him. I didn't want to raise my own voice. I didn't even want to move, in case I gave away our position.

I wanted to curl up and hide like a frightened mouse.

"It didn't need our wristbands, Cheney," he said.

"I know."

"So—so—"

"Maybe only the samplers need our wristbands. Maybe the OTVs are different. Sloan said something about scavengers. Macrophages." I could hear Sloan's voice quite clearly in my head. "Maybe they just . . . go for everything in sight. Maybe they don't differentiate between people, like the samplers do."

Even as I spoke, I was thinking about Sloan. Sloan had run away. He had left us. Not that he could have done much to help—the OTV would have grabbed him if he had—but still I couldn't get that image out of my head: the image of Sloan jumping through the door to the theater. I remembered his comment in the Vaults, too, when he had described himself as expendable. *We all are, to some degree, except Quenby and Arkwright.* Those had been his exact words.

Surely he hadn't decided that *I* was expendable? And Dygall, too?

No. I rejected the notion in horror. No, Sloan wouldn't have left us if he hadn't been forced to. He was a First Shifter; he had a responsibility. He would have tried to rescue us. He was probably trying to rescue us right now.

Somehow, I was sure, he and Arkwright would find us again. They knew what they were doing. They always had.

Not like me.

"What's that noise?" said Dygall.

I listened, but couldn't hear anything except the beating of my own heart and the whistle of my own breath. I could feel something, though. Through my hands and forearms.

Vibrations.

"Someone's coming!" I yipped.

"Shh!"

"It might be Mum!"

"Hello?" A muted hail from somewhere down the shadowy tunnel in front of me. The voice seemed vaguely familiar.

"Who—who's there?" I stammered.

"Cheney?" A different voice. "Is that *you?*"

My heart skipped a beat. *"Merrit?"* I exclaimed, and struggled forward. Luckily the access panel underneath me didn't give way; I passed over it without incident, writhing along like a snake in a sock, until I suddenly found myself face to face with . . .

Haemon Goh.

"Haemon?" I had to blink away tears all of a sudden. The last time I'd seen Haemon, at his birthday party, he'd been a shyly grinning, neatly groomed, perfectly content little nine-year-old. Now he looked like a different boy.

Not that he had been injured, as far as I could see. Physically he was unscathed. But his face had changed forever. It was all eyes—big, black, staring eyes—and beneath the grime and goo, it was devoid of hope.

"Cheney!" cried Merrit. She was right behind Haemon; I caught a glimpse of her collar-spot flashing about as she moved. "Oh, Cheney . . . Oh, Cheney . . ."

"What happened to your ear?" Haemon whispered.

"Nothing." I realized, suddenly, that my ear hurt. But I dismissed the fact without interest. It wasn't important. "Who else is with you?"

"No one," Merrit quavered, and stopped abruptly. I think she had lost the power of speech for a moment. But she cleared her throat at last and went on. "Who's that behind *you*?"

"Dygall."

"Hello, Dygall," said Haemon in a dull tone.

"Hello, Haemon. I figured you'd be in here somewhere."

"Did you?" It surprised me to hear this. If I could have turned around, I would have. "Why?"

"Because Haemon's the air-duct master," Dygall wearily replied. "Didn't you know? He used to spend all his free time in the ducts."

"He did?"

"Sure. Where do you think I got the idea from?"

I stared at Haemon, who stared back at me. Merrit said, "If it wasn't for Haemon . . ." and trailed off again, sniffing.

"I bet Haemon knows exactly where we are," Dygall continued, with a muffled sigh. "Don't you, Haemon?"

Haemon nodded. I realized that he was on his hands and

knees, that he was small enough to turn around inside the air duct. I asked him where he was going, and his bottom lip began to tremble. It was Merrit who finally answered.

"We didn't know where to go," she replied. "We . . . we . . . Oh, Cheney, it was so awful . . ."

"I know."

"We had to get out—"

"You should cut off your wristbands," I interrupted, and heard Dygall's scornful sniff. "It's still worth trying, Dygall!" I said sharply.

"Why?" he growled. "That OTV went for us anyway."

"But the samplers didn't."

"Arkwright was wrong."

"He was not!" Arkwright couldn't be wrong. The very idea made my blood run cold. "CAIP's still got our details on file, remember? It knows what a human being is. Even if it can't recognize individuals, it can still send an OTV after us all! Arkwright wasn't wrong. If we can wipe all references to human beings from CAIP's memory, we'll be all right. We *will*."

"What are you talking about?" said Merrit, and I tried to explain. I tried to explain about the wristbands, and the samplers, and the scent pellets, and the On-board Transport Vehicles. I didn't mention Zennor. I didn't mention Sadira. I told Merrit that Dygall and I were searching for Arkwright, Yestin, my mother, my father, and Sloan. We had become separated, I said. But they couldn't be far away.

"You should come with us," I concluded, and Merrit said, "Where to?"

That stumped me. I wasn't sure. Back to MedLab? When Dygall spoke, he might have been reading my thoughts.

"We can't go anywhere near that . . . that *thing,*" he said hoarsely. "It might bust into the air duct."

"I doubt it." For some reason, I felt that the air ducts were safe from the On-board Transport Vehicles. Don't ask me why. Blind stupidity, perhaps. "Mum probably wouldn't have stayed around there, either . . . I don't know . . . Maybe she went back to the Vaults . . ."

"Do you have something sharp?" Haemon suddenly croaked.

"Huh?"

"You said we had to cut off our wristbands."

We had nothing sharp, of course. Sloan had pocketed the laser-head scalpel. I tried to think, conscious of Haemon's agonized gaze. He was looking to me for help, guidance, comfort, anything.

I wondered what he had seen. Nothing that I wanted to hear about, probably.

"The Infirmary," I finally decided. "We'll go to the Infirmary. That's not too far from here. It's near Pathology, so we'll be heading in Mum's direction, but it won't mean tangling with that OTV again. There's bound to be something sharp in the Infirmary." I peered at Haemon. "Can you find the Infirmary? I'm completely lost."

Haemon hesitated. He looked around with a dazed expression. Then he seemed to focus.

"If we back up," he said to Merrit in his soft little voice, "it'll be quicker."

"Back up?" she echoed.

"To the next junction. We have to turn left. Left, left, right, and left."

"Okay." We had a goal now. A destination. It made things easier. It gave me something to concentrate on. With something to concentrate on, I wouldn't lose control. "Okay, Merrit, you back up until you reach the next junction," I said. "Then keep backing and let Haemon turn left first—Haemon, then me, then Dygall. Then you can go. You can bring up the rear. Okay?"

"O-okay. But—"

"Haemon, when we reach the right access panel, *don't open it up.* Just pass straight over it, and *I'll* open it up. I'm the one who'll be going down. Just me."

"But—"

"*Just me,* Dygall. I'm the oldest. It's my job." Even so, the thought of trying to fill Sloan's shoes made my stomach lurch. I had never been a leader. I didn't think I was made that way. "If there's no one in the Infirmary, I'll come straight back up again with whatever sharp instrument I can find," I continued, "and after we cut off the wristbands, we'll press on to the Vaults. Maybe even to BioLab. We'll keep going until we find the others. Agreed?"

There was a pause. At last Haemon nodded solemnly. "Yes," he whispered.

"Agreed," said Merrit.

"Dygall?" I gave him a shove with my foot.

"Well . . . I guess," he muttered. "But what if something goes for you in the Infirmary? You'll need help then."

"No, I won't."

"Yes, you will."

"All right, Dygall." I wasn't about to argue. "If something goes for me, I want you to jump down and stick your tongue out at it. It's about all you can do, and I'm sure it'll really, really help."

"Very funny," he spat.

"Or maybe you can just, like, throw yourself into its mouth. So it doesn't eat me. That's the only alternative."

"Not if we had a few *weapons*. If we had proper weapons—"

"Well, we don't. Not yet." Knowing that I had been a bit harsh, I added, "But it's on my list, okay? It's something we'll look for. Definitely. Now . . ." I took a deep breath. "Are we ready to go?"

"Yes," said Merrit.

"Yes," said Haemon.

There was a brief silence.

"Yes," said Dygall.

And we began to move.

Chapter Sixteen

It didn't take us long to reach the Infirmary. When we did, I thumped away at the access panel until I pushed it open. Then I stuck my head through the gap to have a good long look around.

To my relief, I saw that every door in sight was sealed shut, undamaged. There were no scent pellets zooming about—just the room's original complement of samplers. They worried me but not much. Though we couldn't really be certain of anything, I was fairly sure that samplers were harmless to anyone who hadn't been scent-bombed first.

I recognized the room, despite all the changes that had taken place. It was part of the High Dependency Unit. I had been there before, years ago when I was visiting Yestin during one of his bad spells. I remembered how Caromy had been sitting at his bedside. She often spent time with him when he was sick, and would stay with him for hours, chatting, reading, and even (sometimes) singing. She had looked up and smiled at me as if she couldn't have imagined a more welcome sight. And I've never forgotten the way it made me feel, because in many ways it was like a mimexis moment in real life: a moment of sunlight and fireworks and vivid, burning colors.

I fell for her then. When I was only fourteen.

But there wasn't any point dwelling on the past.

So I returned to the present, scanning the room for something useful. Though the walls and floor were now a tangle of huge ropy veins, though the quarantine pods were now fluid-filled cysts, some of the equipment had remained untouched. Drugs were piled high on a metal tray. A wheeled trolley containing all kinds of promising drawers had been released from its floor grips. Crumpled insulation sheets were piled in one corner.

"This looks good," I observed. "This looks *very* good."

"Are you sure?" said Dygall, behind me.

"Positive. It's sealed up. The door can't have been opened since the red alert."

"Then go! Quickly!"

I went. I lowered myself through the access hole and dropped onto the floor, which bounced when I hit it. I found it very hard to walk on that floor because it was so corrugated and unstable. I must have stumbled or fallen over about twenty times. But I managed pretty well. I found a pair of scissors in the trolley, along with various instruments that were probably gas-jet hypodermics or molecular deconstructors or something—I didn't know, so I decided not to touch them. The scissors, I realized, would be perfectly adequate. After I'd passed them up to Dygall,

I examined the food dispenser, which was still vaguely recognizable. What I mean is, there was still a definite serving hatch and a sort of menu pad—though the input key was the only real console feature left. (It had turned into something not unlike a giant wart.) When I pressed it, however, nothing happened.

"Damn," I said.

"Cheney!" It was Dygall. His red face was hanging out of the access hole. "What are you doing? Come back!"

"The dispensers don't work anymore!" I exclaimed.

There was a faint, confused noise from in the ceiling.

"Merrit says they do," Dygall related. "Merrit says she used one a little while ago. Haemon had to have a drink."

"Well, I can't make *this* one work." Something struck me. "Shit. The wristbands! I never thought of that."

"Never thought of what?"

"Did anyone ever try to order food without a wristband on?"

We stared at each other, Dygall and I. Then he said, "No one ever stopped wearing a wristband before."

"*Damn* it, Dygall!"

"Look—just come back, okay? Just come back in here, Cheney, *please.*"

"Wait." I'd had another idea. There were several pressure flasks lined up along a bony bulge that might once have been a bench-top. They were scattered among various cryogenic capsules that made my heart leap. What if—? Could it be—?

"Cheney!"

"Hang on, Dygall. Look at this." I fumbled for the nearest flask and checked the label reading. "Liquid oxygen!"

"What?"

"Liquid oxygen! We can use it!" Seeing his blank expression, I almost screamed, "Against the OTVs, you fool!"

"Oh!" Light dawned. "You're right!"

"There's only one, though." The other flasks were empty. There was nothing on their labels except pressure readings. "It doesn't give us much . . ."

"Is there any powdered magnesium?" Dygall queried. "Or paraformaldehyde? Or titanium? Liquid oxygen explodes when you mix it with any of that stuff."

"Don't be stupid. How can we risk an explosion? We'll blow ourselves up." I hurried back to the access panel, the flask tucked under my arm. "With this we can just unscrew the lid and splash it around. Liquid oxygen burns like anything." I was about to say, "It's as bad as acid," but changed my mind. The word "acid" conjured up pictures of Zennor and his smoking face. "It's a killer," I finished, passing the flask to Dygall. "Give that to Merrit. Help me up."

"Is there anything to stand on?"

I looked around as he took the flask. I couldn't use the trolley; it would have rolled out from under me. There was a stool, though, and I fetched that. I was a bit worried about its stability on the mushy floor, but I didn't have much choice.

"Okay," I said. "Just stick your arms down. Come on, Dygall—I told you to give that to Merrit."

"Uh—"

"What? *What?*"

"It's my shoulder," he explained. "You did something to it last time." He rolled it in its socket and winced. "You pulled a muscle or something."

"Oh." I was instantly contrite. "Sorry. I didn't know."

"Maybe I should go forward and let Merrit help you up."

"Yeah, okay. That's a good idea."

It worked, too. Haemon made way for Dygall, who made way for Merrit, who reached down and helped to pull me back into the air duct.

"Merrit? Did you cut off your wristband?" I asked.

"Yes," she replied. By this time, she was behind me.

"Where *is* it?"

"Right here."

"Pass it over, then. Dygall! Tell Haemon to pass me his wristband!"

When I had both wristbands, I dropped them through the hole onto the floor. Then I sealed up the access panel. "Okay," I said when I'd finished. "Let's go. Who's got those scissors?"

"I have," said Merrit.

"Keep them. Dygall! Tell Haemon we're heading for the Vaults!"

"Yeah, I know."

"And be careful with that flask. Don't touch the lid or anything."

"Can I roll it along?"

"Roll it?" I wasn't sure. "Better not. It might hit Haemon's foot. Can you stuff it down the front of your suit, do you think?"

"I'll push it," said Dygall. "Don't worry, it'll be all right."

So, we set off for the Stasis Banks. The trip was a slow one because Dygall was having trouble with his shoulder and my ear was very painful. No one had the strength to talk much. I wanted to find out what Merrit and Haemon could tell me about the rest

((183))

of the ship—about Technical Fault Protection, and the filtration pumps, and the Remote Access Repair Units—but I couldn't bring myself to ask. They both seemed to be in a state of shock; I could sense that they had seen some very nasty things.

In the end, though, I had one question. Just one.

"Do you know what happened to Caromy?" I inquired. "She was in pump station one . . ."

Merrit didn't answer immediately. Up ahead Dygall halted for a moment before proceeding. At last Merrit sighed.

"No," she replied softly. "I never saw Caromy. I was in the Depot."

"Right. Thanks."

I knew that thinking about Caromy wouldn't do me any good at all. So I tried to focus on our immediate situation. Our first priority would be to find my mother—my mother and Arkwright. Our second would be to find more liquid oxygen, or something similar. Our third would be to solve the mystery of the malfunctioning food dispensers. Or should we look for a secure space before worrying about food? Perhaps it would depend on what Arkwright said.

And then there was my father. We had to find him. I refused to accept the possibility that he had been squirted by a sampler or swallowed by an On-board Transport Vehicle. It hadn't happened. It *couldn't* have happened.

"Cheney?" Dygall had stopped again. "Have you noticed something?"

"What?"

"Check out the walls."

I shifted, and my collar-spot illumined a small patch of reddish tissue.

"What about the walls?" I said.

"Haven't you noticed?"

"Noticed *what*?" I was getting impatient.

"They're swelling," said Merrit. "They're inflamed."

"Huh?"

"Look how red they are. They weren't like that before."

Peering down the squashy passage, I realized that she was right. Its lining *had* become a deep, angry red. Not only that, but it was puffing up. It was constricting our space.

"Oh no," I breathed.

"Could it be us?" Merrit sounded hopeless. Despairing. "Could we be irritating the airways? Like dust or gas molecules . . . ?"

"The question is will it get any worse?" said Dygall. He was craning around, peering back over his bottom at me. "What if we get *stuck* in here?"

"Okay, wait." I was trying to put my thoughts in order. "Ask Haemon where we are. Ask him if we're nearly at the Vaults." As Dygall passed on my question, I laid my bare hand flat against the shiny surface that was pressing down on all sides.

It felt warm. Almost hot.

"Haemon says we're about ten minutes away from the Stasis Banks," Dygall reported. "Okay. Well . . . let's try to get there as fast as we can."

We tried. We did our best. But there was the pressure flask and Dygall's shoulder, and as we struggled on, our route became more and more difficult. It wasn't long before I realized that the walls were closing in with a vengeance. I found myself pushing back bulges. Forcing up the ceiling with the top of my head.

I never knew a Shifter who suffered from claustrophobia. We were used to confined spaces. But when it came to being trapped in a wet, clinging bag . . . Well, I don't know anyone who could have put up with that for long.

Dygall was the first to break. "Cheney! We've got to get out of here!"

"Okay. Okay—"

"*Now!*"

"Next access panel. Tell Haemon."

"*Haemon! We're getting out!*"

"Don't let him go first, Dygall! Do you hear me?" I couldn't tell: the billows of red flesh were like a smothering curtain. "I'll check it out myself, okay? Dygall?"

"I heard you!"

The next few minutes were hard to take. Sweat broke out all over my body. I had to *force* myself not to panic. The space in front of me grew smaller and smaller; the encroaching walls pressed my head down, and seemed to tighten around my chest. Finally I couldn't even raise myself onto my elbows—I had to wriggle along like a snake.

"Here!" Dygall squawked at last. "We're here!"

"Good . . . great . . ." I could barely gasp it out. Then I felt the lurching and the thumps. I caught a flurry of movement. "What are you . . . ? Dygall! Let *me!*"

He didn't, though. He punched through the access panel and

shot up through the hole—which opened onto B deck—without even pausing to scan the room above it for OTVs.

I guess he'd had about as much as he could take.

"Dygall!"

"It's okay."

"Are you crazy?"

"I've got the flask, remember?" A pause. "Anyway, there's nothing here. Just a few samplers. The door's sealed." As I pulled myself through the hole, he added, "Do you know this cabin? *I* don't."

It was a single-occupancy cabin, which had probably featured all the standard fittings: bed, Interface Array, bathroom, extension table, storage hatches. Now it was like someone's abdominal cavity: a bag of strangely shaped, oddly colored organs. But some things hadn't changed. There were still pillows, and cushions, and insulation sheets, and several glass bottles, and . . .

"Look!" cried Dygall. "Look at that!"

I was so astonished that I froze in the act of hauling Merrit out of the air duct. There, on the pulsing pink wall, hung a sword and its sheath. The blade was slightly curved and the hilt highly decorated. It didn't look like something you would have found at the Battle of Waterloo.

"It's a *samurai* sword! From Japan!" Dygall exclaimed. "Can you *believe* that?" For the first time since Haemon's birthday party he sounded exactly like his usual self. "It's the real thing!"

"Who the hell was allowed to bring a samurai sword onto *Plexus*?" I said as Merrit clambered to her feet beside me.

"I don't know. Someone from Japan?" Dygall approached the

sword but couldn't stretch far enough to lift it down. "We could *use* this," he said, turning to me. "These swords were *vicious*."

"All right. Hang on." I bent to help Haemon, who was the last person out of the air duct. He then clung to my arm until I gently placed his hand on Merrit's elbow. "It's all right, Haemon," I assured him, noting the way he shied at the sight of a sampler flashing past. "These are only samplers. They can't hurt you unless you've been scent-bombed. Dygall—don't touch that sword. You'll drop your oxygen."

I had to wipe my hands on an insulation sheet before I lifted the sword down from its bony brackets. We were all slightly sticky; our hair was plastered with gummy stuff, and our suits looked as if we'd been rolling in mucus.

It was disgusting.

"Okay," I said, balancing the sword in my left hand, then my right. It was surprisingly heavy for something so thin. "Okay, I'll take this. Dygall can have the oxygen, Merrit can keep the scissors, and Haemon . . . whatever we find next, you can have that."

"But where are we going?" Merrit asked. Her voice trembled. "How are we going to get around? We can't use the air ducts. We can't use the filtration ducts—they're full of fluid."

"What about the cable conduit?" I suggested. The air and filtration ducts ran through the conduit, which provided a kind of outer casing. But Merrit shook her head.

"You'd be climbing on the power cables," she said, hugging herself. "It's too dangerous—especially with a sword."

"Are you sure?" I wasn't convinced. "It's pretty big, that conduit. And it was designed for manual intervention."

"Cheney, we're not properly insulated. Anyway . . ." She hesitated and swallowed. A ghastly expression flitted across her face. "Anyway, there—there are RARs in the conduit . . ."

"Oh."

She had a point. I looked at Dygall, who said, "Arkwright and the others . . . they wouldn't be in the ducts anymore, either. They'd be stuck using streets and tubes."

"You're right." I abandoned the conduit idea. If we used the conduit, we might miss my mother. "We'll have to go back down, though. Back to A deck. We'll have to use the stairs." Realizing how dry and sore my throat was, I crossed to what had once been the kitchen, and picked up a glass bottle. It contained some sort of carbonated fruit juice. When I broke the seal, the hiss made us all jump. "Let's have a drink," I said, setting down my sword, "and then we'll go."

The bottle passed slowly from hand to hand. I don't know why, but something about it—about drinking one after the other from the same bottle—made me think of that moment just before the start of a basketball game when you all clap hands together. Or the point in a war story when a group of soldiers is set to go "over the top." I think everyone else felt it too: the sense of being part of a team, with a job to do, rather than a sad little clutch of terrified kids.

Maybe there was something in that bottle besides carbonated fruit juice. On reflection, there probably was. It certainly left a warm feeling as it trickled down my throat into my stomach.

"Right," I said after we'd drained the last drop. "I'll go first. Dygall can bring up the rear. Merrit, you keep your eye on the ceiling. Haemon . . ." I stared down at him, wishing he didn't

((189))

look so small and defenseless. "Haemon," I said, "you take this bottle. The next hard surface we come to, we can smash the end off it, and then you'll have your own weapon. Okay?"

He nodded.

"Okay." I raised my sword and put one shoulder against a sagging door panel. "Let's go."

Chapter Seventeen

It was tricky, getting through that door. Even with my whole weight pressed against one panel and Dygall's body wedged against the other, we could push open only a small hole not much wider than my head. After Haemon and Merrit had squeezed through—Merrit clutching the scissors in case something horrible was waiting in the street outside—I had to prop the hole open with my sword sheath so that Dygall and I could wrestle our way out of the cabin.

But we managed, at long last. And we were lucky, because no Remote Access Units or On-board Transport Vehicles were poised to grab us. The street was empty, except for a few samplers crawling along the walls.

This was no guarantee, however, that it would *remain* empty.

"Okay," I panted. "Stair shaft."

"Not the lift?" said Merrit as I pressed forward. It was Dygall, however, who replied.

"Are you kidding?" he said. "The *lift?* Who'd be stupid enough to step into a *lift?* They probably have *teeth* by now!"

"Shh." For the first time in ages Haemon spoke. "Don't make so much noise!" he hissed.

I agreed with him. The less attention we drew to ourselves, the better. So we hurried toward the closest stair shaft in perfect silence, save for when Dygall stumbled over a lump in the floor.

The stair shafts were closed off with hatches, but these hatches were very rarely used. Normally the shafts were left open. Only during emergencies were they supposed to be sealed.

The trouble was, our recent red alert had been just such an emergency.

"Dammit!" I said when we reached the first shaft. Its hatch was in place, and its swivel lever now looked like part of some giant deformed ear. I tugged one coil—nothing. I pushed another—no response. Everything was so slimy, I couldn't get a firm grip.

"Let's try the next shaft," Merrit proposed, under her breath.

"At the next junction, you mean?"

"Yes."

I swallowed. The next shaft was down the starboard tube. We would be very exposed out there on the platform.

"Okay," I said. "Let's try it."

I peered around the corner, up and down the tube. In the distance, to our right, I could see a Remote Access Laundry Unit skittering away in a mist of scent pellets. So I decided to head in the opposite direction.

"Down here," I whispered. "Dygall, keep your eye on that RAL, will you? Make sure it doesn't turn around."

Dygall nodded. I struck out along the platform, treading carefully over bumps and ridges and the odd, slithering sampler until I reached the next junction. One cautious peep into this particular street told me two things: first, that it contained no obvious threat (just a distant corpse, lying in a red puddle), and second, that its stair shaft was also sealed shut.

I could have cried.

"Next one," I said softly. "Dygall?"

"We're okay," he reported in a barely audible voice.

"Blue things." Merrit put her mouth to my ear, lifting her scissors to point at the ceiling. "Look."

"It's okay." What else could I have said? "We're not wearing wristbands."

Then I crossed the intersection and made for the one beyond it. By this time the platform was so slick that Haemon nearly slid off onto the tube track. Merrit caught him just in time, though his weight probably would have pulled *her* down if I hadn't grabbed her collar. The scuffle made me nervous; though I wasn't sure how the OTVs located their targets, there was every chance that vibrations might have had something to do with it.

Luckily the next stair shaft had been opened up and left open. One quick glance inside told me that it was empty, though its internal structure now closely resembled a series of ribs fanning out from a central spine. In other words, there was a good chance that one of us might break a leg trying to descend what had once been a perfectly good staircase.

At least, however, we wouldn't be eaten. Or sprayed with acid.

"All right," I said to the others. "You stay here until I've checked outside the bottom door. If it's clear, I'll give you a yell."

"Be careful," Merrit pleaded.

"You, too."

It turned out to be worse than I thought. The stair-ribs were as slippery as glass; they bent under pressure. In the end I gave up trying to stand and slowly bumped down on the seat of my pants—bump, bump, bump. On the way I passed a hatch that made me pause for an instant, desperately clawing at the greasy handrail.

That hatch, I knew, opened into the cable conduit, which lay between A and B decks.

"Cheney?" said Merrit from the top of the stairs. "What are you doing?"

"Nothing. I'm— Nothing." I decided not to inspect the cable conduit. Who knew what might be lurking behind that hatch? Gazing up at Merrit, I added, "You're better off sliding. Just hang on till I give the all clear, and come down *one at a time*. Or you'll smash into each other."

I'd hardly finished speaking before I reached the bottom of the stairs, bumping to a halt opposite the gaping A-deck doorway. Through it, I could see nothing but the wall across the street. Even so, I lifted my sword, clasping its hilt in both hands. Its tip hardly wavered as I climbed to my feet. Slowly, very slowly, I edged around the wall until I was almost hugging the doorjamb. From there I had a view of the nearest junction and part of the A-deck starboard tube.

Nothing dangerous was immediately visible.

Millimeter by millimeter I then poked my head *around* the doorjamb to survey the streetscape on my right. I saw a cloud of milling scent pellets near the far junction and a mutilated door about halfway down the street, but nothing that especially alarmed me. Though I thought I recognized the street, I couldn't be sure. Everything had changed so much.

"Okay." I pulled back into the stair shaft. "Who's first? Merrit?"

"Haemon," she replied. But just as she was settling Haemon onto the topmost rib—"Be careful of that bottle," she advised him—something astonishing happened. There was a wet, popping sound, and the conduit hatch sprang open, slapping against the wall.

"Ch-Cheney?" someone croaked.

I almost died. I almost dropped dead of fright, before I saw who it was.

Inaret.

I recognized her face instantly, despite the fact that it was a deathly color. She was shaking so hard that I could see the tremors even from where I was standing. Her dark curls were smeared with dried gloop.

"My God," I sighed. "Inaret."

"Oh, Cheney . . ." Merrit's voice cracked. She sounded as if she was going to burst into tears.

I knew how she felt. The sight of that little girl fumbling out of the shadows was almost unbearable.

I looked away quickly to check the street again.

Nothing.

"Be careful, Ret," said Merrit from above. "It's slippery; don't fall."

But Inaret had always been clumsy. Though she used the hatch door for support, it was as well lubricated as everything else in that stair shaft, and when her feet shot out from under her, she couldn't get a firm grip even on the handle. She came spinning down on her stomach, her limbs spread wide. I reached her just as she hit the bottom stair.

"Inaret," I said. "Are you all right?"

She didn't answer. Instead, she launched herself at me, throwing her arms around my neck and holding on for dear life. It felt as if she wanted to crawl inside my rib cage.

I could spare her only one hand, though. My other was occupied with the samurai sword.

"Cheney?" Merrit was wiping her eyes. "Is she okay?"

"I—I think so." Physically, anyway. "But I'll have to cut off her wristband."

"Do it, then. Quick."

The Samurai sword was so thin that it slid easily beneath Inaret's wristband, and so sharp that it sliced through the wristband after only half a minute's careful sawing.

Inaret didn't question its removal. She didn't even speak. And when I stood up to make way for Haemon, Inaret came with me. She wouldn't let go. She wrapped her legs around my waist and clung like a bonded atom. I was very tired, but even so, she wasn't much of a weight.

She shook me up badly. I had been trying so hard to focus on the task at hand, and Inaret brought back too many memories. Memories of ice cream spilled on the floor of the Health Center, and clumsy fairies dancing at the annual Christmas pantomime, and Caromy wearing her hair twisted up in two golden antennae. Memories of cold lemonade, and virtual snowfalls, and streams of silvery music. A host of beloved faces flashed into my head—Caromy, Teillo, Sloan, my mother and father. They were laughing or smiling. Their eyes were clear and their skin was clean.

My heart almost burst into a million pieces. Because I realized—with a sudden, cold clarity—that these things belonged to a vanished past.

But I jerked my chin to drive the memories away. I couldn't succumb now. If I did, we were finished.

"It's okay, baby," I murmured, watching Haemon slither to a standstill at my feet. I didn't have a hand to spare, but he struggled upright unaided. "You okay, Haemon?"

"Yeah . . ." Haemon stared at the little girl. "What happened to Inaret?"

"I don't know. I guess she was hiding." I felt her grip tighten. "Were you hiding there, baby?"

She nodded without raising her head from my shoulder.

"It was a smart place to hide," I said.

At that point Merrit joined us, having come downstairs at a more sedate pace than Haemon. She put her hand on Inaret's crusty curls, and said, "Are you hungry, Ret? Are you thirsty?"

Another nod.

"I wonder how long she's been there?" Merrit looked at me. Something had changed in her face; I could see a trace of the old

Merrit, instead of the stupefied, shell-shocked zombie who had been following me around so far. Inaret's sudden appearance hadn't shaken her up. It had helped her pull herself together—I don't know why. "Could there be anyone else inside the conduit?" she went on.

"I can't see anyone!" Dygall interjected, and we glanced around to see that he was hanging off the open conduit hatch, one foot wedged against the rim of the opening, another against the wall. His free hand was clutching the pressure flask to his chest. "It's pretty dark in there, though."

Inaret mumbled something. I didn't understand it because she was talking into my shoulder.

"What's that?" I said.

"I was all by myself . . ." She began to cry.

"Here," Merrit offered. "I'll take her."

Inaret, however, wouldn't be moved. She squeezed so hard that I nearly choked. While Dygall shot down to our level—having missed his footing so that his descent was more abrupt than he'd originally planned—Merrit tried to lure her Little Sister away from me. "Cheney needs both arms, Ret," she said. "He has to protect us with his sword. Don't worry. I'll carry you."

"You'll be safe with Merrit." I coughed, my anxious gaze on Dygall. "Is that flask all right?" I asked him. "You didn't bump it, did you?"

"No."

"Come on, baby, please." I had to be firm. "We can't stay here. It's time to go."

Slowly, with great reluctance, Inaret allowed herself to be

peeled off me. She crawled into Merrit's arms. Freed of her weight, I was able to check the street again.

Our way was still clear.

I took a deep breath and turned my head to survey the little group behind me. Merrit stood there holding Inaret. Haemon was huddled beside Merrit, clinging to her pressure suit with one hand while with the other he gripped his bottle so tightly that his dark fingers were white at the knuckles. Next to him, Dygall, grim-faced, cradled the oxygen flask. His freckles stood out vividly against his stark white skin. They all seemed so defenseless. So horribly, appallingly *young*.

The weight of my burden really hit me then. I realized that I was well and truly in charge—that I had to take care of them because there was no one else available to do the job. I realized that Sloan and Arkwright were not about to come to my rescue. Not any time soon.

The lives of my friends were now *my* responsibility.

"Okay," I said. "I think we're pretty close to BioLab, and Bio-Lab's probably a good source of chemicals—"

"Unless they've already been used," Dygall interrupted. We gazed at each other, and I remembered my last glimpse of Bio-Lab: a battleground if ever there was one. It occurred to me that Zennor's body was still there. Lais's, too, perhaps.

And . . . my father's?

"I don't want to go back to BioLab," Dygall whispered. His expression chilled me. "Do we have to go back there?"

"I thought we were going to the Vaults," said Merrit. "Didn't you say they were safe?"

"They might be." I considered our options. "And Mum might be there, too. On the other hand, there's no proper Interface Array in the Vaults, and Arkwright needed an Array. He *had* to have one." I checked the street again. Still nothing. "You know, the Bridge was never attacked, and the best Array on board is there. If I were Arkwright, I would have gone back to the Bridge."

"But—"

"We have two options," I continued, overriding Merrit. "I can check out the Bridge myself while you guys head back to the Vaults. Though," I added, frowning, "I don't know how you're going to get in, with those double pressure-doors and the air ducts all inflamed—"

"We can't split up!" Merrit exclaimed. "We're not splitting up, Cheney!"

"Yeah." Dygall stuck out his chin. "No way are we splitting up."

"Well—okay." I could understand their vehemence. "Okay, so we'll check out the Bridge first. And if it's empty, I'll take you all back to the Vaults. I reckon there's still enough room in those air ducts for Haemon and Inaret, anyway. Maybe they can take something in with them, to prop open the swollen bits . . . I don't know. I'll think about it."

"What we have to do," said Dygall fiercely, "is fortify ourselves. Choose a room and defend it. With electrical fields and chemical mines and things. A room with a food dispenser, and an Interface Array, and everything else we need."

"Maybe one of the loading bays," Merrit suggested. "They have reinforced walls *and* air locks."

"Or the food processing area." Dygall knew what he was talking about; his mother had worked in that unit. "Some of the compartments there are triple-sealed, and if we can't work the dispensers—"

"Okay, fine." I held up my hand. "We'll fortify. But we can't fortify this stair shaft, so let's talk about it later. When we're a little less exposed." I took a deep breath, fixing each of the others in turn with a long, serious look. "If there's no one at the Bridge," I said, "then we'll stop looking. We'll stop looking, and we'll start fortifying. We'll start taking care of ourselves. Agreed?"

Solemnly everyone nodded.

"Right, then." Sword poised, I gave the street outside one last, lingering glance. "Let's go."

Chapter Eighteen

We were two streets from BioLab, and I was undecided. Should I raid it for more chemicals? Would the gain be worth the risk? In the end, however, I wasn't even given the opportunity.

Because, after crossing the first junction without incident, we reached twenty-sixth street only to discover that it could *not* be crossed. One quick peek told me that.

I jumped back from the corner so abruptly that I trod on Merrit's foot.

"Ah!" she yelped, and I slapped a hand across her mouth.

When Dygall questioned me with his eyes, I pointed. Back. Back to the nearest stair shaft.

We retreated in a panic.

"What? What was it?" Dygall hissed as we piled into the shaft on twenty-fifth street. Luckily it was open. Even more luckily it was clear. "What did you see?"

"Something . . . bad," I replied, my chest heaving. In fact, I had seen an On-board Transport Vehicle. *Two* Onboard Transport Vehicles. One had been consuming the other, for some reason. Had they been fighting? Or had the dead one met its end by some other means and attracted the second OTV simply as a piece of waste to be tidied up?

I didn't know. My fleeting glimpse hadn't told me enough.

"We'll go up and across," I continued. "Come back down on twenty-fourth or something."

"Was it an OTV?" Dygall pressed, and I frowned. I jerked my head at Inaret, who was watching me with round, frightened eyes.

"It's all right," I declared as calmly as possible. "We can take a detour."

"It won't follow us?"

"It was . . . busy," I said. Seeing Dygall wince, I added, "It was cleaning up. They really *are* scavengers. They eat each other, as well."

"Oh."

"Come on."

Climbing up those stairs was no easy job. Like the other flight, they had turned into a kind of greased, uneven slope, almost impossible to grip. I had to exert all my strength just to keep my fingers and the toes of my boots wedged into each yielding surface. I couldn't stop moving, either. If I stayed in one place too long, I would slide out of my foot- or handhold. The only certain mode of attack was to keep jabbing away, hauling myself up in one continual movement.

By the time I reached the top, I was exhausted.

"Right," I gasped after a quick scan of the street outside. "Come on up. Merrit, you'll have to put Inaret on your back."

"How are we going to do this?" She groaned. "It's so *slippery*."

"You don't have to get far," I pointed out. "If I stretch down—like this—you'll be able to grab my hand pretty soon."

"Maybe she should use the scissors," Dygall remarked. He was keeping a close eye on the downstairs door. "Maybe she could stick them into the stairs every so often, and pull herself up on them—"

"No!" I snapped. "God, no!"

"But—"

"You want to sound the alarm, Dygall? That'll do it for sure! We'll have OTVs pouring in from every direction!" Seeing Haemon's terror, I quickly lowered my voice. "It'll be fine," I assured them, staring at their upturned faces. "Merrit, if you can crawl far enough to reach my hand, then Haemon can grab your foot, and we'll do it like that. I'll pull you all up together. In a chain."

I did it, too, but not without an awful lot of effort. It was very hard to brace against that slick, springy surface. Though the others tried to help me, pushing against the stairs with their feet and grabbing at whatever leverage they could, they were still a terrific weight. I had to put my sword down. I had to focus all my energy on dragging them to the top landing, where we finally collapsed in a disordered heap, rubbing wrists and gulping down air. For several minutes I completely forgot about watching the door.

Once again, though, we were lucky. This lapse didn't have any fatal consequences.

Merrit was the first to recover. "Are you all right, Cheney?"

"Yeah . . . yeah . . . in a second . . ."

"Did you hurt yourself?"

"No, no . . ." Actually, each of my arms felt as if it must be at least a meter longer. They didn't seem to want to bend at the elbow. But I flexed them anyway and picked up my sword with trembling fingers. "Everyone okay? Haemon?"

He nodded. Dygall said, "Let's go." I staggered past them both and took up my usual position at the edge of the door. Slowly, carefully, I peered around the corner . . .

And pulled back quickly.

There had been movement. A shape. It took me a second to process what I'd just seen; meanwhile, Merrit nudged my arm. She and the others—they were all wide-eyed. Frozen. Poised to run.

I shook my head.

"Wait," I mouthed, then peeked around the corner again. Sure enough, there was a man crawling along the street. He was wearing a pressure suit and something else . . . something I didn't recognize. At first I thought it might be some kind of cloak, because it hung off his shoulders, trailing along the ground after him: a big flattish, oval shape as limp as a pancake, with two long black cords wrapped around his neck . . .

Suddenly I caught my breath. That wasn't a cloak. That was a street shuttle. The flat oval base, the two black hand-grips—I recognized all its essential features, despite the fact that they were no longer rigid.

This time when I pulled back, I had my eyes shut. I was breathing through clenched teeth. Preparing myself.

"Cheney?" Merrit whispered. I gulped down a lungful of air and let it out again slowly. Tried to be calm.

"Wait here," I ordered.

"No!" She grabbed me, almost dropping Inaret in the process. I shook her off, and she flinched. She must have seen my expression.

"*Stay here!*" I hissed.

They were all staring at me in horror. I don't know what they were thinking. I didn't really care, at that point. I was concentrating on the man around the corner; I had to speak to him.

So I marched out into the street—three strides—and turned to face him.

"Hello?" I said, my sword lifted.

He heard. We were about ten meters apart, and his ears were still functioning. With a huge convulsive effort he raised his head.

His face was a living nightmare. The skin was mottled with purple blotches; his jaw hung open, exposing a swollen gray tongue; his eyes were swimming, not with tears but with some kind of gluey stuff that dripped like honey. They seemed to be melting away.

Even if I'd known him, I probably wouldn't have recognized him.

He was a stranger.

"Oh no!" I couldn't help myself. The wail just burst out of me. "Oh *no,* oh no . . . !"

"*Don't!*" he squawked. "Don't come near!"

"What—what can I—"

"Nothing." He could barely talk. Something—the street shuttle—was draining his life away. I could see it. I could feel it. "Who is that? I can't see."

"Cheney." I sobbed. "Cheney Sheppard . . ."

"Sheppard?" He coughed feebly. The thing on his back seemed to swell with each breath he took. "Tuddor's boy?"

"*Please!*" I cried. Nothing had prepared me for this: not Haido, not Zennor, not Sadira. Nothing. I felt as if I were going mad. As if I was plunging into the head of something sick and inhuman. I couldn't control myself anymore. I wept and moaned. "Please, I've got a sword. Let me cut it off, *please!*"

"Stay back!"

"*Please!*"

"STAY BACK!" He rolled something toward me: a small gray, pen-shaped thing about the size of my thumb. "Take—take this . . ."

I gaped at him stupidly.

"Don't . . ." He grunted and shifted his weight before continuing. "Watch the red switch," he wheezed. "It's got a timer on the fuse . . . thirty seconds . . ."

"What . . . ?"

"Listen." Another cough. He was sagging. Gasping. His tongue was so swollen that his speech was hard to understand. "It's an explosive . . . for breaking rock. From GeoLab. You have to . . . take it to . . . Depot . . . God . . ."

I picked up the hard little object, holding it gingerly. "But—"

"Won't rupture . . . hull but . . . Oh God . . ." Each word was forced out like the cry of a man being stabbed. "Depot's where . . .

((207))

RARs . . . It's making new leukocytes . . . got to be stopped. De-stroyed. No more new RARs . . ."

"You mean, *blow it up?*" I squealed.

"Like a spleen . . ." He sighed, and then he . . .

Well, I suppose you could say he died. Something split. There was a gush of blood-streaked fluid—a great spout—and I screamed, and would have run to him (at least I think I would have; I was in such a state of confusion and despair, I didn't know what I was doing), but I was stopped. Dygall had left the stair shaft. He grabbed a handful of my suit and yanked me away.

"No!" he yelled. It was a shriek of abject fear. "Get back!"

Merrit was still in the stair shaft. She had been keeping the kids there—a smart thing to do. I'm so grateful. So grateful that neither Haemon nor Inaret saw what I saw. *No one* should have to see something like that.

When I glimpsed their terrified faces huddled in the shadows, I came to my senses. I realized that I was carrying a sword in one hand and some sort of mining grenade in the other. I also real-ized that, not ten meters behind me, someone was liquefying—erupting—under the attack of a mutant street shuttle.

This wasn't a good place to be.

"Quick!" I bawled. "Out!"

I had to look back because it was my job. My responsibility. The street shuttle was beginning to detach itself from the corpse of the man it had killed. One long flexible hand-grip was uncoil-ing itself from around his neck.

We didn't have much time.

"Dygall!" I cried as I danced ahead of the others. But I didn't have to explain myself. Dygall nodded; he understood our predicament. To escape we needed to round the nearest corner, at the tube junction. Before we did that, however, I would have to make sure that our way was clear while Dygall watched our backs, pressure flask at the ready.

Please, I prayed to whoever—or whatever—had preserved us so far, *please don't let there be anything. PLEASE.*

And there wasn't. The tube was empty, except for the usual scattering of samplers and scent pellets. I slapped Merrit's shoulder. *"Now!"* I barked. We tumbled onto the platform and ran, with Dygall bringing up the rear. Fear made us fast—too fast—despite the unevenness of the floor. We had a hard time braking when we reached the next junction; Merrit plowed into me, skidding, and nearly pushed me into the street.

"Ow!"

"Sorry!"

"Cheney, *quick!"* Dygall moaned.

I checked twenty-fourth; it was clear. But the door to the stair shaft was sealed shut.

We had to keep going.

I ran straight for the junction ahead, all the while thinking hard. If we couldn't use the stair shaft on twenty-third, I decided, we would have to turn down a street. On the long empty sweep of the tube platform we were sitting ducks. We would have to dodge about a bit. Maybe hide in a compartment . . .

Luckily there was no need to find a compartment. The stair shaft on twenty-third was open. I dived straight into it and didn't ask anyone to wait while I checked the door on A deck. I just slid down the stairs with my sword held straight out in front of me, ready to skewer anything that might be lurking at the bottom. I figured that, with the force of my accelerating weight behind it, my blade would pretty much pierce whatever the ship might throw in our direction.

I landed awkwardly, because both hands were full. Otherwise, nothing went wrong.

There were no OTVs or street shuttles in sight.

"Quick!" I sprang up, narrowly avoiding Merrit. She and Inaret had come down separately, Inaret ending up against Merrit's back. Haemon and Dygall arrived a split second later, much too quickly. As they collided, Dygall dropped the flask.

We all stood motionless, watching it roll, not daring to breathe. But it didn't lose its lid.

Before it had even stopped moving, Dygall pounced on the gently rocking cylinder.

"Okay, wait." I waved them toward the wall, and plastered myself against it, too, shuffling along sideways until I reached the open hatchway. From there I could see part of the street outside. There were some nasty black stains on the pink and yellow floor, but nothing moved. Carefully I poked a very small portion of my head through the yawning space—and jumped at a sudden explosion of noise.

Of *barking*.

It was Bam.

"Is that—" Dygall began. I had knocked myself while jerking back into the stair shaft. Rubbing my temple, I opened my mouth to reply. Bam, however, was quicker than I was. He surged past me, his tail lashing.

Haemon squeaked, clamping himself to my waist.

"It's all right," I assured him. "It's—it's just Yestin's dog . . ."

Yestin. I caught Dygall's eye, and he looked away. What had happened to Yestin?

"Yestin's *dog?*" Merrit was astounded. "You mean, that's *Bam?*"

"Yes."

"But—"

"There's no time, Merrit," I warned, and gently disengaged Haemon. "Keep behind me," I told him, licking my dry lips. "It's all right. He won't hurt you, see? He wants to be friends."

"Cheney, what have you got there?" Dygall was focused on the grenade in my hand. "What did he give you?"

"Later." I pushed on, into the street, making for the tube once more. But Bam was ahead of me. He skipped past, bounding onto the tube platform. When I didn't follow him—when I stopped at the corner—he trotted over to sniff at my heels while I took my usual precautions.

It didn't really surprise me that the tube was clear. Somehow that was obvious from Bam's demeanor.

"Okay," I said, gesturing at the others. We scurried along, unable to catch up with Bam, who seemed to have a knack for moving quickly over the fleshy hillocks and corrugations of the floor. He didn't even pause at the next junction. I did, though.

Again our path was clear.

It occurred to me, as I pursued Bam, that he had some kind of built-in warning system—that he was, in essence, a miniature probe, with all of a probe's "alert" capabilities. This became increasingly obvious the farther we went. Bam would spring carelessly past a junction, which, upon inspection, would prove to be empty of danger.

I was just about to make some comment about this when his behavior changed.

He stopped and began to bark.

Chapter Nineteen

I pulled up short, naturally. Glancing over my shoulder, I saw the others follow suit. There was nothing behind us except a cloud of soaring scent pellets.

"The Bridge," Merrit murmured in my ear.

She was right. We had returned to the Navigation area. How long ago, I wondered distractedly, had I actually left it? One hour? Two hours? I had no idea.

Bam was getting annoyed. He had planted himself in the middle of the next junction and was barking at an unseen menace down the street.

Unless I was mistaken, that menace lay very close to the Bridge.

"Cheney?" Dygall was hoarse and out of breath. I flapped a peremptory hand at him. Now Bam was growling, and I didn't know what to do. Would something attack him? A street shuttle, perhaps? Should we retreat to the nearest stair shaft? If anything reached him at the junction, it was bound to spot us. All it had to do was look to its right.

I was about to turn tail when Bam suddenly disappeared. He charged off down the street, barking furiously. To my surprise, his barking wasn't cut short. It went on and on.

I gazed at Merrit, seeking some kind of explanation.

"Maybe—he's not a threat?" she speculated quietly. "Because he's not human?"

It made sense. But I *was* human, so I didn't imitate the dog. Instead, I advanced with great caution, millimeter by millimeter, until my right eye socket had barely cleared the corner in front of me.

What I saw made my heart turn over.

The door to the Bridge was still untouched, but it wouldn't be for long. There was a lot of activity outside it. One street shuttle was clamped against it already, excreting acids—perhaps?—and another lay in wait nearby. I also spotted an On-board Transport Vehicle and innumerable samplers whirring around like giant insects.

Withdrawing, I sagged against the wall.

"Well?" Dygall croaked. I lifted a finger to my lips; we couldn't afford to make any noise, despite the dog's clamor. Clearly all those transformed vehicles had enraged him. I had seen him dashing about between them, snapping first at one then at another. But they seemed unaware of his presence.

"Get back," I mouthed, gesturing at Dygall. "Back."

Though he frowned, he did as he was told. So did the others. We retraced our steps to the previous junction, where I glanced down the street, looking for an undamaged door. The only burned one, I noticed, was at the far end, near the port tube.

"Here," I said, and headed for the closest compartment. Its door was shut, but I knew what lay behind that door: a kind of storeroom full of mimexis backup hardware, guidance equipment, spare parts, and so forth. There wouldn't be much space, but I didn't need much space.

Just enough for five small people.

"Take this." I handed Merrit my grenade. "Put Inaret down, and take care of this. Haemon? Give me that bottle. Dygall—keep an eye out."

I poked the neck of Haemon's bottle between the two door panels and used it as a lever, pushing open a hole big enough for my free hand. Then I braced myself and shoved as hard as I could.

Slowly the taut mass of muscle tissue yielded.

"Merrit," I grunted, "can you see inside?"

She stooped and peered nervously. "It's dark . . ." she mumbled. "Hang on."

Before I could stop her, she pushed a hand through the hole, triggering some kind of organic biosensor. Immediately the storeroom was flooded with light.

"Merrit!"

"It's okay," she reported. "I mean, there's nothing to worry about."

"Are you sure?"

"I'm sure. But what are you—"

"Right, then." So far, so good. "Just help me, will you? We

need to get in. Pass that thing of yours to Inaret. Inaret! Don't you drop it, baby!"

Without uttering another word Merrit surrendered the grenade and inserted one shoulder into the hole, throwing her entire weight against the other door panel. Struggling together, we managed to force open a space big enough to crawl through. "In!" I gasped. "Everybody in! Haemon!"

But Haemon hung back. He didn't want to go first. It was Dygall who led the way. Haemon and Inaret went after him, though Inaret was very reluctant. Then I stuck one leg through the hole, and Merrit did the same.

"Okay," I said, "on the count of three—"

"We both jump in," she interrupted. "I get it."

"One. Two. *Three*."

We hurled ourselves into the storeroom as the door panels, released of our combined pressure, sprang back to their former positions. Merrit's foot was caught—she wasn't fast enough—but it didn't really matter. The panels were far softer than they had been, and we were able to jerk her free.

"Can you move your toes?" I demanded. "Are they broken?"

"No . . . ah . . ." She was sitting on the floor, rubbing her ankle furiously and blinking back tears. Inaret's bottom lip began to quiver in sympathy.

"Oh no," the little girl whimpered.

"It's all right." Merrit flexed her foot, grimacing. "It's okay, Ret. I'm fine. Really."

Reassured, I turned to Haemon. "Listen. Haemon. I need your help. Are you listening?"

Mutely he nodded. His skin was streaked with a white crust of dried grunge. My own face felt stiff under the same coating. Even my eyelashes were sticky.

"Okay." As my gaze roamed the walls enclosing us, I tried to collect my thoughts. There were lots of loose items in that room, stacked up on open shelves that now looked like gullets. Some of the items might prove to be useful, I decided. "Everybody listen. I saw lot of things hanging around outside the Bridge. An OTV, a couple of street shuttles—"

"We should go upstairs again," Dygall interposed.

"Wait. Just wait. Just *think*." I surveyed the faces around me. "*Why* would they all be hanging around that door? Hmm?"

A brief pause. Everyone wore tired, blank expressions—except Merrit. She cleared her throat.

"Because somebody's in there?" she suggested.

"Exactly. This immune system isn't interested in empty rooms. Why should it be?" I peered at the access panel in the ceiling. "But before we do anything, I want to make sure. I want to make *absolutely sure* that it's worth doing."

"That what's worth doing?" Dygall inquired uneasily.

I looked him straight in the eye. "We've got weapons, Dygall," I said, keeping my voice steady only with a tremendous effort. "We can't just walk away and leave whoever's stuck on the Bridge."

There was a general intake of breath and a shifting of bodies. Merrit whispered, "But Cheney . . ." before trailing off. Dygall, who was standing over me, wrapped his arms tightly around his pressure flask. Inaret stuck her thumb in her mouth.

"Arkwright might be in there. *Mum* might be in there." I had to wait for an instant before continuing. I had to banish an image of Mum from my mind. "Whoever *is* in there, we need them. We all need each other. If we don't help each other, we don't have a chance. Do you see what I'm saying?" Looking around, I searched for the right words. "Everyone's important, not just some people. Look at Haemon. He's small, but we wouldn't be here now if it wasn't for him. That's why we can't leave anyone behind." Seeing Inaret's frightened expression, I hastened to reassure her. "I'm not suggesting we should charge in like idiots. First we have to make sure I'm right. That's why I need you, Haemon." And I pointed at the ceiling. "You might still fit in the air duct. If there's enough room, you can crawl across the street and check the Bridge. See if there's anyone in there. I mean . . . anyone *alive.*" Gazing up into Haemon's face—because he was standing, while I was crouched beside Merrit—I noticed with a pang his missing tooth and all the baby fat in his cheeks. He was so little. So fragile. He didn't deserve this.

None of us did.

"Look, Haemon," I said, rising and clasping his shoulder. "Inaret's smaller than you are, but she can't do this. She doesn't know her way around the air ducts, not like you. You're the only one—we're relying on you."

He swallowed, and nodded.

"It'll be okay," I assured him. "You'll be safe up there—safer than here. All you have to do is reach the access panel in the Bridge and see if anyone's hiding inside. Then come straight back. Can you do that, Haemon?"

"Yes," he replied in a tiny voice.

"Now?"

"Yes."

"Okay." I glanced around, scanning the shelves for something that I could climb onto. Multispectral scanner? No. Suction cleaner? No. There was a polymer box of lenses, but it wouldn't support my weight.

And then I blinked.

"Is that a *stepladder*?" I exclaimed.

It was. A genuine stepladder. Using it, I was able to unseal the access panel, and Haemon was able to climb into the air duct. He reported that, though narrow, it wasn't too narrow for his skinny frame.

"I won't be able to turn around, though," he told me, gazing down from the top of the stepladder. "Does that matter?"

"I guess not. Not if you can move backwards."

"I can move backwards." For a moment he hesitated, then he pulled himself up through the access hole.

Merrit called after him, "The instant it gets too narrow, Haemon, don't keep going! Don't get stuck!"

A short, muffled reply; I couldn't make out what Haemon was trying to say. Once he'd vanished into the air duct, I clambered up after him until I was peering down the murky tunnel, watching his boot soles slowly recede.

I positioned myself there because—I have to admit it—I was worried. I didn't like sending that poor kid down an air duct all by myself. Who knew what might be hiding at the other end?

"You do realize," Dygall remarked, "that if anything decides to burn through the door here, there's no way out. Did you think of that?"

"Doesn't matter," I said shortly. "We've got weapons. We can fight."

Dygall grunted. Merrit said, "There's a lot of stuff in this room. Maybe we can find something else to fight with."

"Good idea." My collar-spot was illuminating my last glimpse of Haemon's busy backside. "Dygall, you watch the door while Merrit does a search."

"Okay."

Merrit picked up a suction cleaner and examined it closely from every angle. "I don't suppose this would be any good," she said. "I mean, I don't suppose the suction's strong enough to disembowel anything."

"Not on this ship," Dygall growled. "It would be against the safety regulations."

"Speaking of safety regulations . . ." I craned around to check on Inaret. "Would someone else take charge of that thing Inaret's holding? You can pass it up to me if you want."

It was passed up to me. I wondered if I should stick it in a pocket, before deciding not to. What if I forgot it was there and sat on it or something?

Meanwhile, Merrit scrabbled through the objects on the shelves and even tried a few stowage lockers—or the honeycomblike things that had once *been* stowage lockers—without success. Before their metamorphosis these units had probably been locked. Now they were sealed beneath a waxy layer that we might have been able to scrape away with our scissors if we'd had the time.

Unfortunately we didn't have the time.

"Here's one of those polymer masks we used last Christmas," said Merrit. "What could *that* be doing here? Why wasn't it recycled?"

"It's probably Yestin's," I observed, and felt a pang in my gut. Yestin. "He might have hidden it. He's always hiding things away in case he ever needs them for one of his robots. He *hates* recycling. His mum once told me she has to clear loads of stuff out of his room every week."

"There's a funny metal thing, too. I don't know what it is."

"Is it sharp?"

"Not really."

"Then we don't need it."

"Oh, look," said Merrit, pulling down a plastic bottle. "This must be so old. It's got a sticky label on it. This is *antique*." She read the label aloud. "Methylated spirits. What does that mean?"

"Methylated spirits!" Dygall's voice was sharp. "Give me that!"

"What's methylated spirits?" Merrit asked me as she held the bottle out of Dygall's reach. "Is it dangerous?"

"It's *flammable!*" Dygall exclaimed. "Give it here!"

"I think it's some kind of solvent." Vaguely something stirred in my memory, but I couldn't pin it down. "Dygall! What's the matter with you?"

"It's a fuel!" He was dancing from foot to foot. "It's ethanol and methanol mixed together!"

"Really?" Merrit frowned. "That would *have* to be against the safety regulations."

"We can make a Molotov cocktail with this stuff!" Dygall cried. As we stared at him, confused, he tried to explain. "We get Haemon's glass bottle," he said, pointing at it, "we pour the methylated spirits in there, we soak a piece of rag in the same stuff, cork the bottle with it, and then, when we light the rag and throw the bottle, it'll smash in a great big ball of flame! They used to do it *all the time* on Earth! Only they used different stuff, like petrochemicals."

"Petrochemicals!" Merrit shuddered. We all knew about petrochemicals. They were a major cause of our having to leave Earth in the first place.

"Yes, but what's it going to smash *against?*" I fretted, turning the proposal over in my mind. "There aren't any really hard surfaces around here anymore. And how are we going to light it? With an electrical current?"

Dygall stopped jiggling.

"An exposed electrical current is going to be hard to engineer," I continued. "We'd have to rip apart that suction cleaner. Or maybe wire up that photovoltaic battery—"

"What we need is a match," said Dygall, scowling. I couldn't believe my ears.

"A *match?*" I echoed. "What are you *talking* about?"

"A match." Dygall sounded defensive. "You know. One of those bits of wood with the combustible caps—"

"Are you out of your *mind?*" Bits of wood? Combustible cap? "Where do you think we are, the Wild West?"

"I was just saying—"

"Next you'll be asking for one of those—what were they called?—those cigarette lighters!"

Merrit began to giggle hysterically.

Dygall rounded on her. "Shut up!" he snarled.

"Listen, Dygall . . ." I tried to suppress my irritation. "You know an exposed flame is the biggest risk this ship ever had to face. You know the whole place is *drenched* in retardant—triple-insulated, friction-proofed, you name it. There are built-in moisture beads everywhere—"

"I know, I know." Dygall waved my protests aside. "But we're not *cavemen*, Cheney! We're civilized people! We should be able to make *fire!*"

"Not on this ship," I said. "Even the rags are fireproof—if you can *find* a rag. All our rags are supposed to be recycled."

"Then how in the *hell* are we going to survive?" Dygall shouted. "Will you tell me that? Huh?"

Survive. It was a terrible word. In the silence that followed I struggled with some sort of answer, while the full horror of our predicament threatened to overwhelm me. I was confounded.

But Inaret wasn't.

"You could use hair," she suddenly piped up.

We all gawked at her in amazement. It was so long since I'd heard her talk, I'd almost forgotten that she could.

"You can set fire to hair," she added awkwardly. "Hair isn't fireproof. I set fire to my hair with a multispectral scanner once." She nodded at the scanner on the shelf. "It was on a laser setting."

Dygall, Merrit, and I exchanged astonished glances. I noticed the way Merrit's hand rose hesitantly to her own long black plait, which was wound around the back of her head.

"She's right," said Dygall. "Merrit, where are those scissors?

((223))

We could use *your* hair. It would make a great wick. The bit at the top—it'll fit perfectly into the neck of this bottle."

Merrit caught her breath. She can't have liked what she was hearing. Before I could offer any words of encouragement, however, I became conscious of a tremor in the duct lining. It was the first movement I'd felt for a good while. Though faint, it suggested that Haemon might be on his way back, and I squinted down the shadowy passage while below me Dygall scurried about, constructing his Molotov cocktail.

He was hacking through poor Merrit's hair when I announced that Haemon was indeed returning. That much was obvious from the way the air duct wobbled about.

"Okay," I said, carefully climbing down the stepladder. With a sword in one hand and a grenade in the other, I couldn't afford to lose my balance. "Here we go. We'll know in a second." Glancing at Dygall, who was stuffing Merrit's plait into the bottle, I demanded, "Is anyone watching the door?"

"I am," said Merrit quietly. Her face was expressionless. Her hair, clipped off level with her earlobes, had fanned out into a kind of crooked pageboy cut. She picked up Dygall's pressure flask, which had been left on the floor. "Don't worry. I'm keeping an eye out."

"Here he comes." With one boot pressed against the lowest step, I held the ladder steady on that choppy, flexible surface. Then, seeing Haemon's feet emerge from the access hole, I slipped the tiny grenade into my front pocket to free up my left hand. "You okay, Haemon?"

"Yeah . . ." Slowly, centimeter by centimeter, he backed into view. He was an awful mess—gluey, creased, and ruffled—but he seemed unharmed. "I'm okay."

"Did you see anyone?"

"Yes."

"You *did?*"

He nodded. I helped him down the ladder, grabbing him whenever he threatened to slip. "How many are in there?" I asked.

"Just one."

"Alive?"

Haemon hesitated. Reaching my level, he turned to face me, his brow furrowed. "I—I couldn't get the panel open," he faltered. "It was hard to see through . . . all cloudy and spotty . . ."

"But you *did* see someone?"

"Yes."

"Was he on the floor?" Merrit inquired. It was a good question.

Haemon shook his head. "He was sitting at the Interface Array," came the answer. "I called, but he didn't hear me." After a moment's consideration Haemon added, "I don't really know if it was a he or not. I couldn't tell. I could only see his back and the top of his head."

"So he was sitting up?"

"Yes."

"Was he moving?"

"I don't know. Maybe. I couldn't see his hands."

"If he was sitting up," said Merrit in a small tired voice, "he has to be alive. Everyone else I've seen . . ." She trailed off, but I knew what she meant. Acid attacks and liquefaction didn't allow you to remain upright. Neither did an On-board Transport Vehicle.

I swallowed twice before speaking.

"Okay," I muttered. "Well, that's it, then. Someone's on the Bridge. We can leave him there, or we can try to save him." I looked steadily from face to face, registering the smudges, the cracked lips, the bloodshot eyes. Dygall was holding the scanner in one hand and his Molotov cocktail in the other. Merrit was clutching our pressure flask. I had a sword and, as a last resort, a grenade.

Even Inaret had a pair of scissors.

"I saw two shuttles and an OTV," I continued. "That's pretty much one on one. But we have to move fast, before more of them come. Before they find *us*." I flexed my shoulders. "What do you think?"

Haemon sighed. Merrit said softly, "I guess . . . you know, if *I* was in there . . ." She didn't finish the sentence, just smiled a hopeless, tremulous smile.

Dygall stuck out his jaw.

"The more we kill," he spat, "the better it'll be." And he raised his homemade incendiary device. "Come on," he said. "Let's do it. Let's get those bastards."

Chapter Twenty

Before we could move, however, a noise from outside the door made us jump.

It was Bam. Yapping.

"Oh shit," hissed Dygall, all color disappearing from his freckled features. "You don't think—"

"Shh!" I was listening. The yapping had stopped. "Bam?" I said loudly.

Another yip.

"That sounds different," I murmured. "It doesn't . . . It's not the same as it was before." I shot a quick look at the ceiling, before turning to Haemon. "Haemon, can you hop back up and check the street? See if there's anything, you know, outside? If there isn't, we'll head for the Bridge."

Haemon nodded wearily. He climbed into the air duct as Dygall, Merrit, and I ranged ourselves in front of the door.

I couldn't see any discoloration or smell any evil smells. But my heart was still knocking against my ribs like a frantic animal in a cage.

"Inaret?" I said. "Baby, you get up there, too."

"Huh?" She goggled at me.

"Into the air duct, okay?"

"But—"

"Do as you're told, Ret!" Merrit said sharply. "It'll be safe up there."

"But I don't wanna leave you!" the little girl whined.

"You'll be with Haemon," I told her, trying to be patient. "You won't be alone. Come on, be good."

"But I've got my scissors!" she protested, at which point Dygall whirled around and snarled at her like a hungry beast.

"Get up there!" he yelped. *"Now!"*

It worked. Poor Inaret shrank away from Dygall before scuttling over to the stepladder and climbing into the air duct. I couldn't spare her much sympathy. I was far too scared.

"This might take a while to catch alight," Dygall remarked, waggling his bottle at me. "And we don't want to be too close when it does."

"Meaning?"

"Meaning Merrit should chuck the oxygen first. If anything is out there."

I shook my head. "No," I replied. "The first assault will be on the door. Acid. When the shuttle burns a hole, I'll stick my sword through it. Nothing easier."

"Yeah!" Dygall's savage pleasure was ugly to behold. There was something almost unhinged about it. "See how it likes *that*."

Merrit certainly didn't. To my surprise she frowned.

((228))

"What if the acid eats away the sword blade?" she asked, and I shrugged.

"There's always the scissors," I said.

"What about that . . . that thing? You know. In your pocket." Dygall skirted around any mention of the man who had ruptured in front of me. "The thing you were given . . ."

"Oh. That."

"What is it, anyway?" Dygall wanted to know. "Some kind of weapon?"

"It's an explosive device," I rejoined, and Dygall caught his breath.

"An *explosive device?*"

"From GeoLab. For mining . . . bringing down rocks . . ."

"That's *great!*"

"Listen, Dygall." I didn't look at him; I was too busy watching the door. But I spoke very clearly and forcefully so he would get the message. "I was given that charge for a specific reason. It's extremely dangerous, and we should use only it as a last resort. *A last resort.* Understand?"

"What's it for, then?" Merrit inquired. "What's the specific reason?"

"Oh . . ." I didn't want to tell them. It was too daunting. Why spread the news that the Depot was now behaving like a human spleen, churning out more and more Remote Access Units? It wouldn't have helped matters. "Let's not worry about that yet."

"Cheney?"

Spinning around, I saw Haemon's face hanging out of the air duct.

"Well?" I said.

"There's nothing." He was slightly out of breath. "Just Bam."

"Oh. Okay." This new information meant that I had to re-arrange my thoughts. It took me longer than usual, because I was so tired. "Okay . . . um . . . Haemon. I want you to stay up there with Inaret," I ordered.

He blinked, then opened his mouth.

"Don't argue." I couldn't take any more arguments. "Just do it. I'm going to close up this access panel, and you can both crawl over to watch us from above the street if you want to. When we're done, we'll get you down. We'll probably use the panel on the Bridge for that."

Glowering up at him, I waited for his challenge. It didn't come. Haemon remained speechless.

"And you can take those scissors away from Inaret," I finished. "I'm going to trust you with them, but you have to be *very, very* careful. Don't hold them while you're crawling along; we don't want you hurting yourself. Or Inaret. Or the ship, in fact. Just stick them in your belt or something. Can you do that?" Another nod from Haemon. "Good." I abandoned my post at the door to climb the stepladder. When I reached the top, I found Inaret's small pudgy fingers clamped around what had once been the snap-lock seal. "Baby," I said, "you're going to have to move your hands. I can't close the panel otherwise."

"Cheney." Her voice quavered. "Don't go."

"I have to. Just for a few minutes."

"But what if you don't come back?" she mewled.

"Of course I'll come back."

"But what if you don't? Cheney, *please* don't go!"

She wasn't stupid. She knew what the risks were, and she

knew that I couldn't make any promises. Nevertheless, when I squeezed her grubby little hand and moved it out of the way, I found a strange kind of strength in the act of reassuring her.

"We'll be all right," I said gently. "You do your part, and we'll do ours, and you'll see—it'll be fine."

Then I closed up the air duct. Merrit and Dygall were already struggling with the door, one to each panel. As these panels slowly split apart, Bam became visible just beyond them. He retreated skittishly, his tail lashing from side to side.

"Right," I said. "Let me go first, and you'll both have to jump through quickly afterward, the way we did before, Merrit."

"Got it," she gasped.

"Dygall, give me that cocktail thing. If you drop it, you're going to lose your plug, and the fuel will spill everywhere."

"O-okay."

He handed over his bottle. It was awkward enough, getting through the hole they'd forced open, because I had to bend double; my sword and Dygall's weapon made it even harder. At last, however, I staggered into the street, where I kept watch during Merrit's countdown.

"One . . . two . . . *three*," she said, before suddenly landing at my feet. The impact of her fall made the floor heave and shudder. Dygall followed a split second afterward, but jumped to his own feet almost immediately. He snatched the primitive incendiary device from my hand.

"What next?" he said, panting. "Cheney?"

I jerked my head. There seemed to be an awful lot of samplers around, and I couldn't tell why. Was it a random crossing of paths or something more sinister? Leading the way to the starboard junction, I was extra cautious on reaching our first turn. I had a nasty feeling that something big might be heading toward us along the tube platform.

But I was wrong. The tube was still empty as far as the eye could see. (Empty, that is, save for a great explosion of samplers and scent pellets that caused me to scan the ceiling warily for Remote Access Laundry Units.) By this time I was in a very peculiar state. I suppose you could say that I was *beyond* frightened. Yes, I was shaking. Yes, my throat was dry. Yes, all my nerves were as taut as the strings on Ottilie's cello. But my mind was crystal clear, picking up every detail and processing it with a kind of fatalistic calm.

I guess I was almost too scared to be scared. The intensity of my feelings had wrung me out. Depleted me.

With a finger to my lips I edged toward the next corner, wishing that Bam would go away. He was making far too much noise, with all his snuffling and clicking. Glancing at my friends, I saw that they were of the same opinion. Dygall was scowling at Bam with bared teeth, and Merrit's expression was one of utter despair.

I was racking my brain for a solution when the dog abruptly provided it for me. Having caught sight—or scent—of the creatures outside the Bridge, he dashed off down the street toward them, barking angrily. It was a distraction of sorts. My hope was that he might divert attention from my own approach. So, after waiting for about twenty seconds, I took another quick look at our target.

The shuttle glued to the Bridge door hadn't yet broken through. The other shuttle was slithering up walls and around obstacles, its flat, oval shape rippling like the body of a manta ray. Beyond it loomed the dark, throbbing OTV, hand-grips writhing, hatch opening and shutting rhythmically.

Bam was practically nipping at its heels—or should I say its rim?—but the dog might have been invisible for all the notice he attracted. The OTV's tentacles continued to wave about languidly. I realized, with a quick intake of breath, that this might be the *very same OTV* that had attacked us in MedLab.

I didn't, however, allow myself to pursue such a grisly train of thought. If Sloan had been consumed—digested—I wasn't about to open my mind to the possibility. Not even the smallest chink.

Pulling back, I turned to Dygall.

"There's an OTV," I began, but my mouth was too dry: I was barely coherent. I had to swallow a couple of times. "There's an OTV," I repeated in a hushed voice. "When your plug's lit, we'll jump out and you should try to throw that cocktail thing *into its mouth*. Okay? While I keep it busy."

"What about me?" Merrit whispered.

"You come with us." I could barely force the words out through my constricted throat. "There are two shuttles. One's busy with the door—maybe I can deal with it myself. The other one's down to you." Seeing her uncap the pressure flask and unscrew its inner lid with trembling fingers, I added, "Try not to waste any."

Silence fell between us. I could hear a volley of barks from around the corner. Tensely I clasped my sword hilt in both hands, lifting the silvery blade. I could actually see the pulses beating in Merrit's lips and in Dygall's blue-veined forehead. He switched on his scanner, whereupon it hummed to life, emitting a needle-fine stream of bright particles. This beam made quick work of the shiny black rope at which it was directed. Within two or three seconds Merrit's chopped-off plait began to curl and smolder.

"Okay." I looked up. Our eyes met. I realized that Merrit and Dygall were going to do whatever I asked, without a single question or protest. They had entrusted me with their lives. And the guilt I felt—the guilt and fear and sorrow—were so terrible, so sickening, that I almost welcomed the chance to act. To move. To stop feeling and start doing.

"Now," I said.

I hurled myself into the open. Ran at the OTV. Swung my sword. Dygall was beside me; Bam went into a frenzy; the thing ahead was a huge shadowy blur. When my blade struck it, the impact was harder than I'd ever imagined. I'd expected something soft and yielding, like jelly. Instead I hit a dense hide that, while flexible, was as tough as reinforced rubber.

I pierced it but only just. As I wrenched my sword free, the OTV reared up or swung around—I'm not quite sure. It all happened so fast. One flashing tentacle grazed my face, knocking me over. Dygall grabbed me.

"*Run!*" he screamed.

For a second or two I stumbled along backwards, trying to find my feet. Then I lurched upright. Dygall released my arm. There was an awful smell and a fine, almost supersonic, whistling noise. I nearly tripped on the rolling pressure flask, which Merrit had dropped. I'd just had time to register that it was open when a flash of heat made me look around again.

The OTV was pitching and tossing wildly. Through its flanks I could see an orange glow, which quickly erupted into visible flames that licked from one of its open mouths and singed its lips. The shiny black casing crumpled and smoked. All of a sudden it began to collapse in on itself. As the fire was smothered, the monster died. It was still twitching, but its guts had been burned away. It had swallowed Dygall's Molotov cocktail.

The smell was so bad, I could hardly breathe.

Merrit seized me and jerked me around. Though she was saying something that I could hear perfectly well, it didn't make sense. I couldn't process it. I could still see, however—well enough to realize that the free-ranging shuttle was badly damaged. Merrit's liquid oxygen had splashed across a good forty percent of its outer surface, leaving shriveled, purple-gray scars and bubbling blisters. It was writhing around in a puddle of its own bodily fluid.

The other shuttle hadn't moved. It was still doggedly trying to eat its way through the Bridge door.

"I'll do this." I coughed. "Stand back."

I think Merrit snatched at me, but she was too slow. I flew toward the unmarked shuttle, yelling. With every kilojoule of energy that remained in my arms I drove my blade into its carapace—which was far thinner and more elastic than the OTV's. A blunt-edged blow wouldn't have done much; it would simply have reshaped the mass, creating a dent for the briefest of moments. But my weapon was sharp enough to cut. It split the skin, and out poured a great gout of yellow slime. I hacked again as the shuttle fell off the door. I hacked and hacked. I was shouting and crying. Yellow and red stuff slopped over my suit. The smell was beginning to strangle me.

"*CHENEY!*" screamed Merrit. "*LOOK OUT!*"

I whirled around but in the wrong direction. I was facing Merrit, and she was pointing over my shoulder, open-mouthed. I turned on my heel and saw another OTV. It was heading down the street. *Tearing* down the street toward us. Those things could move so *fast!* They were so big, yet they could move so fast!

"*Shit!*" I screeched—and in my panic to escape I slipped in all the liquid underfoot. I fell to my knees. "*Run!*" I bawled. "*RUN! RUN!*" I jumped up, but the thing was practically on top of me. I spun. I swung. Yellow droplets splattered as I wielded my wet sword. It connected, and the shock ran straight up my arm. Bam was barking. Someone was shrieking. Pulling my weapon free, I saw the dog dive straight past me, saw it fasten its jaws around the lip of the OTV's yawning mouth and dangle there for an instant—before being sucked into the maw.

I slashed again madly. Then I was pulled off my feet. There was a tentacle wrapped around my ankle; I realized this as the mouth in front of me flexed open wide. The lips peeled back. I reached for my pocket. The grenade! *Last resort!*

At which point something—a blow—knocked the breath from my body. The light from my eyes.

And there was darkness.

Chapter Twenty-one

"Cheney. *Cheney.*"

Someone was holding me, cradling my head. When my vision cleared, I saw my mother. My mother's face.

It was caked and smeared with dry muck, and the hair was gelled into choppy peaks, and the eyes were red, but it was my mother's face.

I opened my mouth to speak and found that I couldn't.

"It's all right," she murmured, her voice breaking on a sob. "You'll be all right. Oh, Cheney . . ."

My heart was skipping along in a very peculiar manner. I suddenly remembered where I was, and stiffened. The muscles in my limbs, however, responded sluggishly to the demands of my brain.

Mum was stroking my cheek.

"Shh," she said. "Give it a minute. It's the shock. You caught the edge of it."

The shock? What shock? Where was the OTV? I tried to lift my head, without success. Then Dygall's face appeared above me, red and beslobbered.

"Is he all right? Is he all right?" Dygall kept repeating. He clasped my hand in both of his and pressed it against his chest.

This pressure seemed to be coming from a long way off, through several layers of fabric. But when I checked, there was nothing lying between his skin and mine.

What was happening to me?

"It seems to be affecting the peripheral nerves," my mother said to someone out of sight. "But that should pass."

"Are you sure?" said a voice—and I caught my breath. It couldn't be . . . it wasn't possible . . .

"Dad?" I croaked. I turned my head, and there he was. Standing over me, with some kind of long metal stick in his hand. He looked incredibly old, and there was an oozing burn on his face, but it was him. It was really him.

I started to cry.

"Dad . . ."

Mum pulled me up and hugged me ferociously. Dygall, who was kneeling beside her, had to let go of my hand. He stood up. From my slightly higher perspective I could see Merrit hovering alone some distance away, her eyes fixed nervously on the distant starboard junction. A dark, glistening mound rose up behind her, utterly motionless. But . . .

"Where's Haemon?" I discovered that my tongue could move more freely, though my voice was still hoarse. "Where's Inaret?"

"They're still up there," said Dygall, pointing. Mum's grip tightened.

"Haemon?" she echoed. *"Inaret?"*

"They're in the air duct," Dygall explained, and Merrit added from where she was standing, "They should be right up here. Behind the access panel."

"Holy hell," said my father, and vanished from my field of view. Thankfully I was recovering at a rapid pace. My hands no longer felt as if I were wearing gloves. My neck was no longer stiff. I struggled to a sitting position and saw that my father had crossed to the nearest air-duct access panel. He looked at it, then looked around.

"Merrit," he began, "if I lift you—"

"I'll pull it open," Merrit finished weakly. "But someone had better keep watch . . . just in case . . ."

"I will," said Dygall.

While Dad and Merrit struggled with the access panel, my gaze drifted away from them, across the scene of carnage that surrounded us. The street was a mess of lurid color. One shuttle seemed to be smeared across several meters of floor; the other lay structurally intact but perfectly still, its blisters gleaming. Near it the first OTV had shrunk in size. Its singed and flattened shape was smoking a little.

The second OTV hadn't been reduced to such a pitiful condition. In fact, it was moving. One tentacle quivered slightly. One mouth twitched.

"Mum . . ." When I tried to point, I couldn't quite make the half fist that was necessary. My fingers wouldn't close up that far.

So I waved them instead.

"It's all right, dearest," Mum said. "That OTV's done for."

"What—how—"

"An electromagnetic charge. Your dad found a marvelous thing in GeoLab. It's a kind of extendable torch, for lighting up crevices or peering down holes. But when he took off all the safety shields and reset the charge, it made a wonderful weapon."

"Tuddor zapped that OTV," said Dygall, without looking at us. "He trashed it with one blast."

"GeoLab!" I suddenly remembered. The grenade. I fumbled around in my pocket. "Mum . . . there was a man . . . He said he came from GeoLab . . ."

"Oh yeah." As Dygall's glance swept from the port to the starboard tubes, alert for any sign of trouble, he tried to explain. "We met a man—we didn't know him— You didn't know him, did you, Cheney?"

"No." I produced the little gray object. "He gave me this. It's an explosive device."

"*Tuddor?*" Mum's voice was suddenly sharp. She looked over to where Dad was helping Inaret down from the air duct one-handed. In the other hand he grasped his gleaming weapon.

Haemon was already out. He stood pressed against Merrit, his face buried in her chest, his arms encircling her waist. She was patting his back.

"What?" Dad grunted. He wore a strange, bleak expression. Inaret wound herself around his upper body.

"Didn't you say something about sending Beniah out to the Depot?" Mum sounded hesitant. "Something about blowing it all up, to stop it from producing more RARs . . . ?"

"Yes, I did. What about it?"

There was a pause. Mum turned to me. I said, "Beniah didn't make it to the Depot, Dad." And I lifted the grenade.

Dad shut his eyes for an instant. His whole body seemed to sag. Within seconds, however, he had recovered. He squared his shoulders and his back straightened. The lines around his mouth were firm again.

"I'll take that," he declared, striding toward me. Shifting his grip on the baton, he plucked the explosive device from my open palm. Then he slipped it into his pocket.

Meanwhile Inaret continued to cling to him like an adhesive.

"Cheney!" Merrit suddenly spoke up, her voice pitched high. "Cheney, *look!* Dygall, look! It's *Yestin!*"

I was so fuddled, I didn't know what she was talking about. I just blinked. Dygall jerked around, but Mum didn't stir. Dad said, "Yestin? It's okay. You can come out now."

I craned my neck to peer behind me, toward the starboard junction. As I did so, Dygall cried, "Yestin!" Even Inaret turned her head, lifting it from my father's breastbone.

Yestin was emerging from the open stair shaft. I couldn't believe my eyes. Though limping, he was otherwise unchanged: still thin, still crooked, still colorless. It was like seeing a ghost.

"Oh, *Yestin!*" Merrit sobbed. She started toward him, breaking Haemon's grip, and the three of them ended in a tangle just a few steps from the junction. "Come back here!" Dad barked. "Don't wander off; you should always stay together!"

"Yestin . . ." I mumbled, and my mind started to work again. I looked at Mum. "Sloan!" I gasped. "Where's Sloan?"

"Oh, Cheney." Her lips trembled. When her eyes filled with

tears, my fingers closed around her arm. They were working perfectly at long last.

"Where is he? What happened? *Mum!*"

"We had to leave the air duct," she quavered. "After we escaped from MedLab, we tried to look for you, Cheney, but the duct was swelling—"

"I know that!"

"—So we had to get back down, somewhere near BioLab—"

"What happened to him? *Tell* me!"

"I'm telling you, Cheney." She caressed my stiff hair. "We were in the tube. Sloan had the scalpel—he was in front, and he saw the OTV first. He told me to run, and I ran. We hid in a stair shaft, Yestin and I—"

"An *OTV?*" I moaned. "Oh no . . ."

"But Sloan didn't follow us. Arkwright must have turned back as well. I didn't know what to do . . ." Mum's voice, which had firmed up, began to wobble again. She wrapped her arms around me. "Oh, Cheney," she faltered, "I'm sorry. I'm so sorry. I just didn't know what to *do*. I had Yestin . . . I had to get away . . . We went upstairs, and your father—your father was there. He had his zapper, but when we went back to look, that thing was . . . it was already eating Sloan's . . . there was nothing we could . . ." All at once she was crying, weeping into my neck. She couldn't even finish.

What little strength I had left seemed to drain from my body. Sloan was gone. He had abandoned us. He had faced down an OTV with a laser-head scalpel—and he had lost.

All that courage . . . all that brilliance . . . It had been consumed like one of his pet microorganisms.

((242))

How was I going to survive without my Big Brother?

"He can't be dead," I whimpered. "He can't be *dead!* Not *Sloan!*"

"Cheney, listen." It was Dad, leaning over me. He took my chin in his hand. I saw that he was no longer holding Inaret. "We can't do this. We don't have time. Are you listening? Cheney? Comet, get him up. *Comet!*"

I'd never heard Dad talking to Mum like that. To me, yes— once or twice—but not to Mum. When she failed to respond, he hauled her up himself. His face could have been cast from solid steel.

"Come on," he said, releasing her hold on me. "Get up, Cheney. We can't stay here."

"Why *not?*" Mum wailed. "Where are we supposed to *go?*"

"Stop it." Dad spoke brusquely. "Get a grip; you heard the boy. Beniah didn't make it. We've got a job to do. If we disable the Depot plant and finish off the other units with this . . ." He waved his extendable torch.

"With *that?*" Mum's laugh made me flinch. "Are you insane? Do you *know* how many shuttles there are on board this ship?"

"What would you suggest, then?"

"You want to drag all these *children* off to the *Depot?*"

"Of course not."

"So, you want to *split up?* You want to take the only weapon and *go?* How am I supposed to defend them if you do that?"

"You wouldn't have to defend them, Quenby." Dad was talking through his teeth. "They can obviously defend themselves."

I couldn't believe it. They were arguing. They were both alive, and they were *arguing!*

"What are you doing?" I cried. "What's the matter with you?" I was on my feet now, but my knees felt like fluffy insulation fiber. "Don't shout at each other; that won't do any good!"

Dad stared at me for what seemed like ten minutes—though it must only have been a couple of seconds. It was the first time he'd spared me much more than a glance since my awakening. I saw the strain around his eyes, and the rigid set of his jaw, and the terrible seeping wound on his cheekbone.

He reached for the back of my head with one hand, pulled me toward him, and planted a bruising kiss on my brow.

"You're right," he said, letting me go. "No shouting. No arguments. We'll do this by the book. Input first, before we make our decisions. Anything important you kids want to say? About your weapons, maybe? They seem to have been pretty effective."

As Dygall gave him a rapid account of the liquid oxygen and methylated spirits—as Merrit kept watch for approaching danger—I cast around for my sword. It was lying near the electrocuted OTV, which was still subject to the odd nervous tremor. I edged toward its slack tentacles with great caution, retreating quickly once I had retrieved my precious blade.

Though daubed with gummy stuff, the sword was otherwise undamaged. There wasn't a scratch on it.

I was amazed that something so old could have been manufactured so well.

". . . I see," Dad was saying when I rejoined him. "In other words, you're out of ammunition."

"There could be more," Dygall remarked. "We didn't have time for a really *good* look."

"There's certainly more liquid oxygen in MedLab." Mum seemed to have recovered, to some extent. She spoke clearly and forcefully. "In BioLab, too, I'll bet."

"And we cut off our wristbands," Dygall interjected. "It seems to work against the samplers . . ."

"Oh, I took care of that long ago," said Dad, holding up his naked wrist. I noticed that he barely looked at us but kept scanning the junctions on either side. We were in a very vulnerable position. I wasn't surprised to see him so jumpy.

The mention of wristbands, however, set me thinking. I wondered how—and when—he had cut his off.

"Dad," I said, "how did you escape from BioLab? How did you make it to GeoLab? What happened to the others?"

Dad hesitated. He dragged his gaze back from the closest junction and fixed it on me. I saw him swallow.

Mum said, "Later, Cheney. This isn't the time." But Dad was already talking.

"I should have gone with Beniah," he said quietly, almost as if he was addressing himself. "We should have made up our search party *after* the job was done. It was my fault. All my fault."

"Tuddor—" Mum began.

"If you want to know, Cheney, I was lucky." Dad's tone was harsh. "After Lais copped it, and Ottilie, and Firminus, it didn't take me long to ditch my wristband. Good thing there weren't any OTVs around. I didn't encounter one of *them* until I was breaking into GeoLab."

"Tuddor." Mum raised her voice. "The kids don't need to hear this. It's not *useful*."

((245))

Dad blinked at her.

"What we need to do now is work out our next step," she continued. "Are we going to blow up the Depot, or look for liquid oxygen, or fortify the Stasis Banks, or what are we going to do?"

And then I remembered.

I don't know why it hadn't crossed my mind before. Perhaps the electric shock had affected my memory.

"Wait!" I gasped.

They all turned to stare at me.

"In there!" I gestured at the Bridge. "There's someone in there! We have to get him out!"

"Oh!" Merrit, too, had clearly forgotten. "Yes! That's what we were doing! We have to help him!"

Dad frowned. "You mean—"

"Are you sure?" Mum interrupted. "How do you know?"

"I saw someone through the access panel," said Haemon weakly. He was still hovering near Merrit.

"The shuttles were trying to get him," I finished, and became suddenly aware of my parents' troubled expressions. "What?" I demanded. "What's wrong?"

"You mean, this was all a rescue attempt? What . . . what you just did?" Mum stammered.

"Yes." I didn't understand her. I didn't understand why she reached for me and kissed my sticky scalp.

I didn't understand why, after remaining so stern for so long, Dad's face crumpled as if he was fighting back tears.

"We have to do something!" I said urgently. *"Now!"*

"You're right." Dad cleared his throat. He glanced around. "We have to get this door open. Quenby?"

"I'll do it," Mum agreed with a sniff. "Dygall, could you help me, love?"

Dygall moved to lend a hand. They threw themselves against the springy door panels while Dad put his free arm around my shoulders. With the other arm, he continued to cradle Inaret.

"You can help Merrit keep watch," he said to me. "She'll concentrate on the port junction while you watch the starboard."

"Okay."

"If you see anything—*anything at all*—you tell me. I'll take care of it. I'm fully charged over here."

"Yes, Dad."

And then Inaret screamed.

Chapter Twenty-two

We all saw it instantly. We couldn't miss it.

A shuttle, at the port junction.

"In!" shrieked Mum. *"Get in!"*

She was heaving at a Bridge door panel. Reaching for Inaret.
The shuttle was heading our way.

Dad's torch began to hum. He pushed me toward the Bridge.

"Go," he said.

"I've got a sword—"

"Go!"

Inaret went tumbling through the hole that Mum and Dygall
had forced open. Haemon was next in line. As he bent to scramble after Inaret, Dad lifted his weapon. The shuttle was almost
upon us.

I should have wiped my sword. This was the thought that
flashed through my brain: *I should have wiped my sword.* But,
slimy though it was, I raised it anyway. I took a step forward
until I was shoulder to shoulder with my dad.

Perhaps it was a stupid thing to do. Dad's zapper had enough power in it to wipe out a dozen shuttles; what did he need me for? The trouble was I didn't think. I acted instinctively.

While Yestin followed Haemon through the door, I braced myself to meet the shuttle's attack. I was so stupid. It never occurred to me that I might get another electric shock if I struck at the same time as Dad. But that didn't matter, because all at once . . .

. . . it passed us by.

It glided straight past without pausing. *Whsst!* Stepping back, we watched it career toward the starboard junction, past the Bridge, past Merrit, oblivious to our presence. Then it turned a corner and disappeared.

There was a long silence.

"Maybe . . . maybe it'll turn around?" Merrit finally whispered.

"I don't know." Dad's astonishment showed on his face. I had never seen him at such a loss. We all stood there gaping—Dad, Merrit, and I—until Yestin's brittle voice broke in on our stupor.

"Quenby?" he said from inside the Bridge. "I—I think you'd better come here."

Mum gave a little start. She was still wedged against a door flap, holding it open, so she only had to turn her head to glance inside.

Next thing, she was struggling to enter. "Merrit!" she exclaimed. "Merrit, hold this door open for me, will you? Give Dygall a hand."

I looked up at Dad.

"Should that have happened?" I asked.

He shook his head slowly.

"I thought those shuttles were like . . . like Natural Killer cells," I went on. "That's what Mum said, isn't it? Why should some attack us and some not bother?"

"I don't know, Cheney."

"Do you think they've heard about your zapper somehow? Do you think word's gotten around?" Receiving no reply, I added, "They can't be using our wristband signals to locate us. Beniah wasn't even wearing one, and he was killed."

Dad lifted his shoulders. Though his mouth opened, no sounds emerged.

It was Dygall who spoke.

"Uh—Tuddor?" he gasped, red-faced from holding the door for so long. "Tuddor, Quenby wants you."

She was inside. But Dad wouldn't follow her until everyone else had. He took over Merrit's station, throwing himself against her side of the door and nudging her through the hole. Then he relieved Dygall, placing his foot where Dygall's shoulder had been. He had his back pressed against one door panel and his foot pressed against the other. I don't know how he did it. He must have been far stronger than I'd realized.

He told me to crawl under his bent knee, and I did as I was told, squirming awkwardly onto the Bridge after I'd thrown my sword in ahead of me. I flapped about helplessly for a moment, before Dygall helped me up with his free hand. I instantly noticed his sick expression.

"What?" I asked, whereupon he jerked his head. Across the room Mum was attending to someone—someone who sat on what had once been a chair. I recognized the man's long neck. His hunched, narrow shoulders. His lanky limbs . . .

"Arkwright!" I exclaimed.

Behind me Dad echoed, "Arkwright?"

As I sprang forward, however, Dygall grabbed my arm.

"Don't," he choked. "You don't want to see . . ."

It was too late, though. I had already seen. I had seen the filmy cataracts over the eyes. The lolling head. The web of filaments attaching one hand to the Interface Array—or what was left of the Interface Array. My mother had turned away from it, covering her mouth.

"Oh God," she whimpered. "Tuddor . . ."

"What?" Dad had climbed into the room. "What's happened?"

"He—he—"

"Is he dead?"

"No—I—I don't know—"

"You don't *know*?"

"Tuddor . . ." Her voice cracked. "He's plugged himself into the Array."

I caught my breath. Merrit moaned. Dad said sharply, "Well, unplug him, then!"

"I—I can't—"

"What do you mean, you can't?"

"He must have used that old intravenous cannula." Mum was practically whispering. Her hand had moved to her forehead. "I can't believe it. That thing was a museum piece. He must have seen it in the surgical theater—"

"What are you talking about?" Dad was beginning to lose

control. Perhaps he had seen the way Arkwright's body was half submerged in slightly swollen tissue. "Will you get him the hell *out* of there?"

"I *can't!*"

"Why *not?*"

"Because he's part of it now!" Mum cried. At which point she spun around and vomited onto the floor.

When Inaret whimpered, I drew her close. Though half of me was in shock, the other half seemed to be functioning. I knew exactly what had happened. I knew exactly what to do. I gave Dygall a poke in the ribs. "Haemon," I said. "Yestin. Out."

"He—he was trying to access CAIP," Yestin croaked. "Cheney—"

"I know. Come on. Merrit? Bring Haemon. We can't stay. There's no point."

"But—"

"It's too late," I said softly. "Don't you see? He's done it."

"Done what?" my father demanded. "Would someone please tell me what the hell's going on?"

He stood there, disheveled, confused, exhausted. He looked so old.

It occurred to me that he wasn't as well informed as the rest of us. Not about Arkwright, anyway.

"Arkwright wanted to wipe our details off CAIP's database," I informed him. "But he couldn't access the programs. Now he has."

"Oh, Cheney . . ." Merrit sobbed.

"It must have just happened," I continued with a dawning

sense of wonder. Slowly I scanned the faces around me: Merrit's, a mask of agonized guilt; Dygall's, taut and chiseled and stripped of all softness; Yestin's, as white as salt. Inaret's was turned up to me—at the sight of her wide eyes and flushed cheeks something that was wound tightly around my heart abruptly unraveled. I bent and gathered her against me. I started to shake.

"That's why the shuttle went straight past," I murmured. "Don't you see? It can't detect us anymore. It doesn't have the target information. It doesn't know we're human beings." A wild, unwieldy sensation was bubbling up inside; I found myself kissing Inaret's hair, again and again. "We don't exist anymore!" I blurted out. "We're invisible! They can't see us!"

Dad wasn't convinced. "You can't be sure of that," he protested.

"No," I had to concede. After all, I didn't have proof. Just a deep-rooted gut feeling. "No," I said, "but I'll be sure soon."

Then I made him open the door for me and waited. I didn't have to wait long. Only three minutes elapsed before an OTV arrived to clean up the mess outside, failing even to notice me as it slowly consumed one shattered carcass after another.

By the time it had finished its work and moved on, Dad was ready to believe the unbelievable.

We were safe, at last.

The battle was over.

Epilogue

A long time ago *Plexus* was our servant. It did whatever was required of it. It obeyed our every request and was designed to provide us with every comfort. We were the masters of this ship. It was our support and our instrument.

There are some who believe that this fact should be forgotten. To recall it, they say, is to cling to a delusional and dangerous vanity. We are no longer the masters here. The processes of this ship no longer revolve around our needs, like planets around a sun. We are now merely parasites, dependent on whims and loopholes. The food produced, at irregular intervals, by the dispensers on board does not appear for the purpose of feeding *us*. It is there to maintain some kind of balance in the complex systems that keeps this great creature functioning. The cleansing capsules in the bathrooms release their rays and exfoliating scrubs not for our benefit but for the benefit of *Plexus*. If we happen to be present during an unscheduled release, then we can count ourselves lucky.

We are of no importance here and should take care to remain that way. As long as we live unregarded, like the bacteria in our own guts, then we can continue to live. Dwelling on a distant past won't help us to survive. On the contrary. For our peace of mind, such as it is, we must put aside any hope of a return to the Golden Age by forgetting that it ever existed.

This is what they say, some of the Second Generation Shifters. They know nothing of the old *Plexus*. They grow impatient of the First Generation, and our fading memories. Some of them never even met my father, though most can recall my mother. She lingered long enough to see us build a life of sorts. She even delivered my daughters—and helped to rear them. She taught Merrit to be a mother; Inaret, too, when her time came. And Siri, another Shifter who miraculously survived. We found Siri hiding in a cargo bay much later. I report this as a footnote, because Siri didn't play much of a part in the battle we fought.

Neither did Caromy. We never discovered what had happened to Caromy. All we know is that she perished, along with one thousand four hundred and eighty-six other human beings.

She lives only in my memory now. My memory of a past that some of us have already rejected.

Dygall's sons, for instance: they've rejected it. They don't want to hear about the old days or about Earth; they're interested only in the present. Perhaps they're wiser than I am, those tough little urchins, with their hard mouths and unreadable eyes and their father's blazing red hair. Perhaps they're right to challenge my leadership. I've made mistakes, I know that. Perhaps I've wasted time and energy trying to restore conditions that I should have abandoned the moment we lost control of *Plexus*.

But one thing I do know: I'm right about this chronicle. This is no vain and purposeless exercise. This is the history of our people. And if, as I suspect, *Plexus* ever responds to its ancient programming, drawn to the first habitable planet that it reaches, then my grandchildren, or great-grandchildren, or great-great-grandchildren, will need this account and all its appendices. There's nothing useless about the knowledge that I have scraped together here. We can't afford to abandon the little we've recovered about geology, and philosophy, and the navigable universe. This knowledge is the sum of our humanity; without it we're little more than the OTVs and shuttles and RALs that share the ship with us (tolerantly enough, now that we no longer exist).

So I have placed on record this story of our transformation. It's a moral tale, to some degree. We have learned, most painfully, that our command of life was built on fragile foundations—that pride, in effect, comes before a fall. That there will always be change, no matter how hard you might strive for stability. And that, like me, you may have a destiny you can't escape.

Be warned, all of you.

Life is a force that cannot be tamed.

About the Author

Catherine Jinks is a medieval scholar and prolific author for teenagers, children, and adults. Her books have been published to wide acclaim in Australia and overseas and have won numerous awards. She loves reading, history, films, TV, and gossip, and says she could write for eight hours straight every day if she had the chance. Catherine lives in the Blue Mountains of New South Wales with her husband and daughter.